W9-BDG-199

An

①

	DATE DUE		

*For Mary Pollack, of blessed memory,
inspiration for the Mary in this story*

BOOKS BY SONIA LEVITIN

BEYOND ANOTHER DOOR

THE MARK OF CONTE

RITA THE WEEKEND RAT

REIGNING CATS AND DOGS

ROANOKE: A NOVEL OF THE LOST COLONY

SMILE LIKE A PLASTIC DAISY

THE YEAR OF SWEET SENIOR INSANITY

A SEASON FOR UNICORNS

THE RETURN

Books about the Platt Family

JOURNEY TO AMERICA

SILVER DAYS

ANNIE'S PROMISE

Annie's Promise

by Sonia Levitin

ALADDIN PAPERBACKS

"Far Away Places,"
by Joan Whitney and Alex Kramer.
Copyright 1948 by Bourne Co.
Copyright renewed.
All rights reserved. Used by permission.

First Aladdin Paperbacks edition May 1996

Copyright © 1993 by Sonia Levitin

Aladdin Paperbacks
An imprint of Simon & Schuster
Children's Publishing Division
1230 Avenue of the Americas
New York, NY 10020

All rights reserved, including the right of
reproduction in whole or in part in any form
Also available in an Atheneum Books for Young Readers edition
The text of this book was set in 12-pt. Times Roman.
Printed and bound in the United States of America
10 9 8 7 6 5 4 3 2 1

The Library of Congress has cataloged the hardcover edition as follows:
Levitin, Sonia, 1934–
    Annie's promise / by Sonia Levitin. — 1st ed.
      p.   cm.
    Summary: Her experiences at a summer camp in the California mountains
in 1945 give twelve-year-old Annie Platt new insight into her overprotective
family of German-Jewish immigrants. Sequel to "Silver Days."
    ISBN 0–689–31752–2
    [1. Camps—Fiction. 2. World War, 1939–1945—United States—
Fiction. 3. Family life—Fiction. 4. Jews—Fiction. 5. German
Americans—Fiction.] I. Title.
PZ7.L58An   1993
[Fic]—dc20   92–16819

ISBN 0–689–80440–7 (Aladdin pbk.)

Contents

Faraway Places

LOOKING BACK, I CAN SEE THAT THE WORLD EXPLODED THAT summer, 1945. It was a time of pain and of victory, for the country and for the world. But I was twelve, going on thirteen, and I hardly noticed the howling winds of change, for the changes in me seemed ever so much more real.

That year a certain popular song kept coming on the radio, and as I listened to the song I imagined the glamorous possibilities.

"Far away places with stange sounding names,
Far away over the sea,
Those far away places with strange sounding names
Are calling, calling to me."

As I skated along the street, with my dog Skippy running beside me, I hummed that song and tried to imagine such places as Africa, China, and Siam. In grammar school we had studied Africa; I loved seeing pictures of the vast veld, the wild animals, and those beautiful, dark-skinned people.

That spring the gas station on the corner gave away beautiful prints of the national parks. I collected all of them, marveling at the rivers and pine forests I'd probably never see. Of course, because of the war, gasoline was rationed. Papa needed all his gasoline for work; he certainly wouldn't drive us to a national park. Besides, it would never occur to Papa to leave his work long enough to take us.

Friends from school talked about fishing and camping with their families. One of the girls had a tent. I thought about that as I sat high in the olive tree in our backyard. From there, I could see up over the rooftops. I had never been to the country, never seen a farm or ridden a horse, although I'd read dozens of books about them, imagining myself the great heroine who tamed the wild foal or nursed a sick newborn colt back to health.

We lived in a five-room rented house on a fairly busy Los Angeles street. All the corners were taken by shops—a large market, a drugstore, a flower shop, a dry cleaning shop. It was not a good place for kids, as Mama often said, but it was convenient, with a bus stop on the corner and a garage in back that Papa had converted into a workroom.

I longed for a gang of kids my age, so we could play capture the flag on summer nights, or hide-and-seek or kick the can. But there was only Patty around the corner, a few little kids, and some tough-looking older guys. Patty could be sweet as pie and let me ride her bike, or she'd get nasty and tell me to drop dead, for no reason.

Summer was coming. My really best friend, Marjorie, was going to spend two whole months with her cousins on their farm in Wisconsin. I'd read just about everything Louisa May Alcott wrote, including *Eight Cousins*. I envied Marjorie, those cousins, and a whole summer on a farm. I'd have given anything to go with her.

But Papa had plans for me. He wanted me to work for him, sewing satin linings into fur collars. Papa designed and sold coats. When he wasn't out selling, he finished the coats out in the garage, sewing on labels and fur collars, preparing them for shipment. He was always "short on help," as he said. Since Lisa and Ruth had jobs of their own, I was the only one left. Of course, I'd known how to sew since I was seven. But it just wasn't my idea of a great way to spend the summer.

Mama also had plans for me. I could do all the marketing and keep the garden weeded. No wonder I longed for faraway places! But my only transportation was roller skates or the city bus, and since my illness, Mama didn't let me go far.

I had been in the hospital. You'd think I'd lost an arm or a leg, the way Mama hovered over me. What happened was, I'd had my appendix out two months earlier.

Papa worried and slid his hand over his sleek hair. "*Eine Schande*," he kept saying. "A shame," although whether he was ashamed of me or of my weakness I wasn't sure.

Things were not smooth between Papa and me. I was the wild one. I heard him say it often enough to Mother, through the crack of the kitchen door as I stood in the hallway listening.

"She is growing up wild," Papa said. "Always running. Climbing like a boy. No wonder she is sick all the time."

"Arthur, Arthur," Mother gently scolded him. "How you exaggerate! She had an inflamed appendix. Is that caused by running?"

"Who knows? Maybe. You think it's good what she does? All night, she sits up reading instead of sleeping—I know. I see the light under her door. I go in, and Lisa is fast asleep, but Annie is reading, reading. All day, she is in trees or on roller skates. Where in heaven's name did she get roller skates? What kind of a thing is it for a young girl?"

Softly Mama said, "I also skated when I was a girl."

"You, Margo?" I heard Papa laugh.

"Oh, yes. I skated so fast through the streets of Berlin that I beat the streetcar to the corner!"

I was amazed and delighted at the thought of my mother on roller skates, speeding after a streetcar! But then Mama sighed and said the sad German words, "*Es ist Alles vergangen,*" which of course I understood—*It is all vanished.*

We were American citizens now, but still, my parents usually spoke German, especially in times of crisis. To me, the language was ugly. I wanted to shed my German self like an unwanted skin.

When I got sick, of course, they all jabbered in German, and Papa called my sister Ruth, who was at nursing school. Ruth had become our family adviser on all medical matters.

"Annie's in pain!" Papa shouted into the telephone in harsh German. "She can't stand up. What should we do?"

Ruth gave directions from across town, where she lived in a rooming house near the hospital. "Have her lie down. Is she vomiting? Have her put her knee to her chest," Ruth advised, "and see if that hurts."

As Mother instructed, I gingerly bent my knee and brought it slowly toward my chest. I let out a yelp of pain—"Ah!"—and felt my whole body contract.

"When did it start?" Papa shouted. He waved his arms.

"Tell me! Tell me! What's wrong?" He strained toward me, and I saw the pulse throbbing at his neck. I started to cry.

"Get out, get out, Papa," Lisa yelled. "You're scaring her to death. Papa, you are terrible when someone is sick, always shouting."

Papa retreated, shaking his head and looking embarrassed. Lisa was the only one who could talk to Papa that way. She was his favorite and had always been.

Lisa sat down on my bed. I tried to smile at her, but I felt a terrible twisting, searing pain in my middle.

"How long have you had pain like this?" Lisa asked. She wore a beautiful emerald green sweater that lit up her blue eyes. People said we looked alike, but my hair was darker, and Lisa was very graceful and stylish, a typical dancer, while I favored jeans and a cowboy hat.

"For a few months," I admitted. "I guess since January." The pain would sneak up on me at any time of the day or night, without respect for what I was doing. Sometimes it came when I was in the bathtub, sometimes while I ironed my clothes. I told Lisa, "Today on the way to school it was awful."

All morning I had struggled through classes, fighting the pain and the nausea, until finally I staggered to the office and confessed it. "I'm sick."

"Why didn't you tell us before?" Lisa asked.

I shrugged. "I don't know," I whispered. But I knew. I didn't want to be sick, I didn't want to be in bed.

At last Dr. Belzac arrived.

Mother bustled around, looking flushed and excited. Dr. Belzac was also Mama's employer, the father of little

Daphne, the child Mother had been looking after for some time now.

Mother handed Dr. Belzac one of our best linen towels, newly laundered, as she ushered him toward the bathroom, where a brand-new bar of soap lay ready on the freshly polished sink. "Here, Doctor," Mama said in a queenly tone. "You will want to wash your hands."

The doctor finally came in to examine me. Papa was banished to the living room, where he turned on the news, playing the radio softly out of respect for the doctor; but still, we heard rumblings.

Mama stood beside the bed. Lisa watched from the door. The doctor laid his hands onto my stomach and gently he pressed.

I nearly leaped off the bed and gave a piercing scream that brought Papa tearing through the hall, wild-eyed. "What is it? What is it?"

"Acute appendicitis," the doctor said, snapping his stethoscope into his bag. "It's a good thing you called me. She needs surgery. The sooner the better."

"Would you do it, Doctor?"

"No, no. This is not my specialty. But I know a wonderful young doctor whom I highly recommend. Dr. Cronin. Herbert Cronin. I'll call him immediately if you like."

So it was arranged. No respite. No time to call Marjorie or Barbara. Just pack a little bag with my bobby pins and a couple of paperback books, a pair of pajamas, a toothbrush, and a hairbrush. I snuck in a little sample tube of my very own lipstick, Tangee Natural, which the lady at the drugstore had given me just the day before.

If Mama saw the lipstick she'd skin me alive! Well, I

thought, reconciled, at least I was getting away. The hospital might be an adventure. I'd never had an operation before. Maybe I'd get presents!

Let me tell you, an operation is no fun. They knock you out with drugs so strong that you feel as if you've been hit by a log. Next thing you know there's a sour taste in your mouth and people are whispering, poking you, sticking thermometers in your mouth, asking silly questions like, "How are you?"

Well, I acted, Mama later said, like an outlaw.

"How are you feeling, Annie?" the handsome Dr. Cronin asked, smiling down at me.

"What do you think, you idiot!" I yelled, still under the influence of the drugs they'd given me, and in pain.

"You sound all right," the doctor said, and I glimpsed a grin.

"What are you laughing at?" I yelled. "It's no joke!"

"You'll feel better in the morning. How about a sip of water?"

"Get out of here!" I hollered, and, as they told me later, I knocked the glass clean out of the doctor's hand and across the room, where it shattered against the wall.

Later, when I came out of it, and the nurses told me how I'd behaved, I was devastated. "What? I did that?"

"Worse," said a young nurse, laughing, holding her hand over her mouth. "Oh, you cussed them all out, you threw things. We had to take everything off your little table."

Mortified, I blushed and turned my face to the wall when Dr. Cronin next came to see me.

"Annie!" he called. "You're looking grand." He squeezed my hand.

The pressure of Dr. Cronin's large, warm hand sent sparks through my body. I glanced sideways, saw the firm set of his chin and that wonderful smile. He was the handsomest man I'd ever seen, not counting Tyrone Power and Clark Gable. But this was no movie star on the screen, but an actual man holding my hand.

"What a horrible experience," I grumbled. I was hugely embarrassed by my terrible behavior. And I was aghast at the feelings that shot through my body now, feelings I'd never had before. I was sure the doctor could feel my pulse beating in my hand, and that he knew how I felt.

Quickly I pulled my hand away, as if in anger.

Dr. Cronin's smile vanished. "I'm sorry I made you so uncomfortable," he said. "Surgery isn't pleasant. But you're young, and you'll recover very quickly. Wait and see."

With that he turned and went out into the hall. All night I envisioned his face as I turned my head from side to side. My body was too sore to move. The next day I got up and tried to walk. I felt as if a rope had been tied around my middle.

After that, I stayed home for a week and then went back to school. But something was wrong. Something in me wasn't working properly, as if in the surgery I'd lost more than my appendix.

I started to feel funny in the mornings. Woozy. Dizzy. My head would ache in a single spot, over my right eye or at the temple. The ache would grow into a pounding, and I would see horrible spots leaping before my eyes, and I'd try to hold on to the things I knew—my name and address, my age, my very being—for it felt as if everything real was slipping away from me into darkness.

"Migraine," Mama would whisper. Dr. Belzac had given a name to these headaches. "Poor Annie."

Mother would bring an ice pack for my head.

My family gathered in the hallway outside my room. They whispered about me. "Shh! Don't go in there. She's asleep. Sick again. I don't know. . . ."

"*Eine Schande*," Papa moaned. "A shame."

"Why is she still sick?" Lisa asked, her voice edgy with anxiety. I thought maybe she was sorry for all the times we fought, for making me turn off the radio, for not letting me borrow her new sweater.

I heard Mama's heavy tone. "She's simply not strong. We have to be careful. We can't let her overdo."

They brought the radio into my room. I was allowed to listen for an hour in the morning, after everyone left for work, and an hour each evening, no longer. "You must not get overstimulated," Lisa explained.

Lisa was kind. She made cocoa for me. She brought me a fashion magazine, *Vogue*, and we leafed through it together, but I wasn't really interested. I couldn't care less about fashion—she was the one who loved clothes. Not me! I wanted to be running in the fields, wearing blue jeans and boots, catching a horse around the neck, feeling the wind in my hair.

But I was stuck in bed, then in the house, and finally back at school; I felt like a zombie. Except for Marjorie and a couple of other friends, nobody seemed to care that I'd been gone for nearly a month, or that I had changed.

How? I'd stare at myself in the mirror; I couldn't actually tell. The change seemed to be coming from deep within.

On the morning of my return to school, my counselor,

Miss Broderick, told me, "If you need anything, Annie, just come and see me."

"Thank you, Miss Broderick," I said. I'd rather die than confide in her, even if I could figure out what to say. What could I tell her? That I was in love? With Dr. Cronin? That I longed to be grown up and beautiful and important?

Sometimes I lay awake at night while Lisa slept in the bed beside mine. Then I'd wonder, What's wrong with me? Why aren't I good at anything? Why can't I ever hit a home run? Why can't I think of anything to say to Larry Steiner? When will I get myself into a bra?

One morning in May a message came for me in homeroom. "Annie Platt, you're wanted in the counseling office."

What now? I hurried to the office. I loved the sound and the feel of the halls between classes, when the long corridors gleamed. The showcase on the wall held trophies for people who excelled in sports or debate or scholarship. My dream was to win such an honor someday, but it was as far away as those places in stories and songs—China, Africa, Siam—words, only dreams.

I opened the door to the office.

Miss Broderick smiled up at me. "Come in, Annie! Sit down, sit down. How are you doing?"

"Fine, Miss Broderick."

"That's grand. Listen, I have an idea for you. An opportunity. Have you ever been to the mountains? Would you like to go to summer camp?"

I shook my head. Might as well ask if I'd ever gone parachute jumping from a plane. "The mountains?" I echoed. "Summer camp? Where?"

"Several hours from here. San Jacinto Mountains. It's a

beautiful area, Annie, with pine trees and a lake. The campers sleep in log cabins, and they have all sorts of activities and sports—wood carving and playacting, hiking, swimming, horses—''

"Horses?" I cried. "Horses?"

Miss Broderick laughed lightly. "I take it you'd be interested in going this summer?"

"Oh, Miss Broderick!" I cried. "Oh, yes!"

The counselor put some papers together and slipped them into a folder. She handed it to me, saying, ''Have your parents take a look at this, and if they agree, have your mother or dad call me to make arrangements.''

And in that moment it struck me. They'd never let me go.

2

Breaking Away

MARJORIE AND I WALKED HOME TOGETHER, AS ALWAYS. I told her about seeing Miss Broderick and being invited to go to camp.

"Lucky you," Marjorie said. "How long will you stay?"

"It's almost five weeks," I said breathlessly. Once again I looked at the pamphlet Miss Broderick had given me, although I had already memorized the information. "Look, it starts on Friday, June twenty-second and ends July twenty-fifth. Almost five weeks!"

A lifetime, it seemed like. Five weeks in the mountains! Marjorie understood my excitement.

She looked at the pamphlet and said, "Look, they have a lake and horses and everything. You could learn to ride. You could swim every single day. Annie, it'll be the best summer in the world!"

I nodded, choked with conflicting emotions. Yes, yes, it would be the best summer in the world, with new friends, faraway places—but now those mountains seemed as distant as China and Siam. "They won't let me go," I said, my voice already quavering with disappointment.

Marjorie pulled back her hair, let it down again. "Why wouldn't they let you go?" she asked. Her tone was reasonable, just as her parents were reasonable.

I sighed. "You know my folks. Everything is a federal case."

Marjorie laughed. "You're funny, Annie. They'll let you go. Your sisters will stick up for you. I bet you'll make so many friends at camp."

"I wish you and I could be together," I said. "I'll miss you."

"But you'll meet all these new kids! It says they're from all over the city. Look, it's coed. That means boys."

We laughed, and I felt giddy. "Sure," I said. "That's the best part!"

Marjorie and I talked a lot about boys. Sometimes we called them on the phone, disguising our voices. Naturally, we never did it from my house.

Papa said our phone was only for business. That's what I mean. Everything at my house was complicated, a federal case. I longed for the mountains, for freedom.

A car with an open top came roaring along the street. It was filled with high school boys, whistling and screaming and singing at the top of their lungs. "Hey, the Yanks are coming, the Yanks are coming—it's almost over over there!"

Marjorie and I looked at each other. For weeks we'd been hearing rumors on the radio that the war with Germany was almost over. On Saturdays at the movies we saw newsreels of people fleeing and German cities in ruins from Allied bombs.

"Do you think it's really true?" I asked Marjorie. It seemed like a miracle.

"I hope so. My brother will come home," Marjorie said with a smile.

"And Ruth's fiancé," I added. "Peter. They'll get married, maybe they'll have a baby. I'll be an aunt."

"When this war is finally over," Marjorie said in a sing-song voice. We'd been hearing that for years, but still it went on and on and on. We saw the liberation of France in the newsreels, too. The French people sang and danced in the streets. Strangers even hugged and kissed each other. Girls tossed flowers to the soldiers and people drank champagne.

"I'd better hurry home," I told Marjorie, going at a trot. "Piano lesson. Tuesday."

"Call me later," Marjorie said with a wave.

"Sure," I said. If Papa was in a good mood I'd make him laugh. "I need the phone," I'd say. 'I've got business with Marjorie—monkey business."

I hurried down the street, so as not to be late for my lesson. I'd be perfectly virtuous, do all my chores, never argue or answer back for at least a week. Then, seeing how well behaved I was, my parents might let me go to camp.

Last week I'd gotten a difficult new piece, a Chopin étude. It was beautiful. My teacher, Paula, had played it for me. Then I asked her the question I had been considering for months. If I devoted myself entirely to the piano, and practiced four or five hours a day, might I make it as a concert pianist?

Paula hesitated, then shook her head. "I doubt it, Annie. Most professional musicians begin at three or four years of age. It's rather late for you. You're nearly thirteen."

"When I was four," I said heatedly, "we were worrying about the Nazis. Nobody had time to think of music lessons."

"I know, Annie," Paula had said. "But be honest with yourself. You have so many interests. Could you be completely committed to the piano?"

Paula knew me; she was right. I had too many irons in the fire.

Now I bounded up the front porch, and as I pushed open the front door I yelled, "Skippy! I'm home!"

"Quiet!" My father's sudden shout startled me. He sat in front of the radio, a cup of coffee balanced on his knee, and bent close to the speaker, listening. The announcer's voice was clipped and tense. ". . . and with Allied victory in sight, Hitler is said to have committed suicide in his bunker. . . ."

I stared at Papa. I could read nothing, neither hatred nor grief, on his face, though I know he felt both. His entire family, since the Nazi takeover, had disappeared.

"Is it over?" I whispered.

"Soon," he said, holding up his hand. He squinted, as if he were in pain.

I whispered, "I'm supposed to have a piano lesson. . . ."

"No," Papa said briefly. "Your teacher called. No lesson."

"But why?" My teacher never canceled a lesson, except in extreme situations.

"*Quiet!*" Papa said again.

So it was probably true. Paula would be sitting in front of her radio, too, waiting for news. And then! I imagined how we would celebrate, laughing and singing. Maybe we'd go out on the street and people would begin dancing and kissing each other—for years we'd dreamed of this time—when the war is over!

But there were still chores to do. In the kitchen I found Mother's shopping list and a ten-dollar bill. Carefully I tore the necessary meat stamps from the ration book, and also stamps for sugar and butter, just in case any was available.

Quickly I changed into my jeans and T-shirt. Mama had, of course, objected to the jeans, but I'd bought them with my own money, so she couldn't complain.

Mother had picked them up with a grimace. "A girl wants to look like a boy?" she said. "The material is so stiff! I don't understand it. Pretty soon, I suppose, the boys will wear dresses?"

"All the girls are wearing these," I tried to explain.

"You aren't 'all the girls,' " my mother retorted.

I made Skippy stay on the porch while I ran across the street to the market. The produce section was wide open to the sidewalk; at night an iron gate was pulled across the opening. A couple of years before, when I'd had two rabbits, they sometimes escaped from their pen and made their way across the boulevard to Von's Market. Ray, the manager, would call me on the phone. "Hey, kid, come on over here and get your rabbits—they're eating up my lettuce and radishes!"

Now I walked past the produce to the back and found Ray. "Any butter today?" I asked.

"Nope. One miracle a day is enough. Looks like it's gonna be over for sure this time. Pretty soon we'll get all the butter and cheese and meat we want. I'm fixin' to buy me a new car when this war is really over."

For years, everything was on hold. Nothing was produced

that wasn't for the war effort; food disappeared from the grocery shelves. It was being sent to our troops overseas.

"Do you suppose your folks will go back there?" Ray asked.

"Back where?" I asked

"Why, to the old country. Germany. Maybe they have property there."

I shook my head, sickened at the idea. I never wanted to go back to Germany. Did we have property there? I didn't even know.

Quickly I made my purchases and ran back home. "Papa!" I called, pushing open the front door. But he was gone.

I found him out back in the garage, sitting there with pins sticking out of his mouth, his brow furrowed deeply as he pinned up the hem of a coat.

Papa's large fingers handled the cloth deftly. He finished pinning the hem, and without looking at me asked, "You came to sew a collar?"

"No. I have to do the dishes and start dinner. I just came to . . ."

"Shoot the breeze?" Papa asked, half smiling. He loved slang. He reached for a cigarette, lit it, and exhaled deeply.

"Is it over, Papa?" I asked.

"Not yet. Almost." He had a small radio on the shelf; we heard murmurs, then music.

"What will happen?" I asked.

"What do you mean?" Papa still squinted, moistened the end of the thread, slipped it easily into the needle, and began swiftly to stitch. His needle strokes were rapid and precise.

"When the war is over, will we go back and find our relatives?"

"Back to Germany?" Papa looked astonished. "Never! No people are left over there anymore," Papa said bitterly. "The humans fled. Or they were murdered. The pigs are left."

"But, won't you go and look for your . . . your mother? Your brothers?"

"I don't have to inquire," Papa said grimly. "I know what happened."

"What about Clara?" I asked. "What about the baker next door to us? He used to give me cookies. They weren't Jews. They might still be alive."

Papa stared at me. "How do you remember all this? You were so little!"

"I remember Clara," I said, "and the swings at the park. The rest is—terrible."

"Yes," Papa murmured. "Terrible." Papa drew hard on his cigarette, then waved the smoke aside, a strong gesture. "Look, I have no pity for the Germans. I cannot. We have lost too much. As for me," he said, and I saw the tension in the hollows of his cheeks and his throat, "I will never set my foot back on German soil. Never. Our life is here now."

I felt a strange mixture of relief and sorrow.

A volley of barking interrupted us; Skippy streaked out to the yard. Ruth stood at the back door, wearing her white nurse's uniform and cap. She looked very tired.

"Annie, is there anything to eat?" she called.

'There's some pound cake in the pantry," I called back, and I went to her.

An uneasy truce hung between Ruth and Papa; last week

she had left in the middle of a raging fight. Papa did not want Ruth out on the streets at night. "I don't want you out alone after dark," he had yelled. "People will think you are a common . . ."

Defiant, Ruth had yelled back, "I'm twenty-two years old, Papa, and tired of being treated like a child. Leave me alone! I have enough to worry about without you persecuting me!"

Now I went into the house, and I sat with Ruth while she ate a slice of Mother's pound cake. Golden yellow, baked with carefully hoarded eggs and butter, the cake was moist and delicious. Tiny pieces of grated lemon peel glistened from the cake. I helped myself to a glass of milk and cut myself a piece. Ruth drank coffee, strong and black. She lit a cigarette, flicked the ashes into her saucer.

"Mother says you should use an ashtray."

"Mother isn't here now," Ruth said. "I wish people would stop criticizing me," she added crossly.

"I'm sorry."

Ruth sighed deeply. "Me, too. I guess I'm on edge. I haven't slept much lately."

"How come?"

She gave me a bemused look, then smiled slightly. "Don't you know? We sit up late and listen to the war news on the radio. All of us have boyfriends or fiancés over there. In the morning we grab the newspaper to look at the casualty lists. Every day I hold my breath until I see Peter's name isn't on the list. And then I worry again, because I know he could already be dead. The lists are incomplete. Sometimes they're weeks late. And if anything happened, who would tell me?"

"His parents, I guess."

"Maybe. I called them once."

"You called his parents? You called long distance?"

Ruth nodded. "His mother sounded very nice. She called me 'dear.' She said, 'When Peter comes home, maybe we'll get to meet you, dear.' "

Ruth stubbed out her cigarette. She finished her coffee, then sat staring into space, biting her lip. I could see, too, that her fingernails were bitten down to the quick.

"Want to play chess?" I asked. I knew the answer.

Ruth shook her head. "I think I'll just lie down awhile."

I did up the dishes, pressed the hamburger into patties. We were allowed only one pound of meat; I filled it in with flour, oatmeal, one precious egg, and lots of chopped onions. Then I set the table in the dining room. Tonight would be like old times: five for dinner. Often Lisa ate out now with friends from the bank, or with her boyfriend, Nate, and Ruth only came home once a week.

I ran out back and picked three lilies from the side of the garage, where they grew in profusion.

"Is Ruth all right?" Papa called to me. He stood at his packing table, folding coats into tissue paper.

"Yes. She's just tired," I said. Both Papa and Ruth were stubborn as mules. I wondered how long they'd sulk. Papa never apologized for anything.

Inside, I arranged the lilies in a glass, and suddenly Ruth came bursting into the room with such a shriek that I nearly dropped everything. "It's over!" she screamed. "It's official, I just heard it on the news! Oh, my God, he'll come home!"

Moments later our telephone rang. It was Mother. "It's

over!'' she cried into the telephone. ''Have you heard? Let
me talk to Papa.''

A few minutes later Lisa called. ''Have you heard? Germany surrendered. Unconditional surrender. Everybody's going crazy here—they're throwing paper scraps out the
windows—I'm coming straight home.''

Cars honked outside. Radios up and down the street were
on full blast. Everybody sat glued to their radios, amazed,
speechless. Our boys, our brave American boys, were coming
home at last, victorious. Oh, it was true that we still had to
fight the Japanese, but Hitler, the tyrant, was dead, and that
was cause for celebration.

That evening we all sat at the table, and we could hardly
eat. A strange, eerie reluctance hung over us. What could we
talk about? For years victory had been our dream; now the
Nazis were beaten. But they had taken half our world with
them. We could not really celebrate.

Softly Mother said, ''Dr. Belzac has a nephew fighting
in Europe. They are very relieved now.''

''Marjorie's brother will be coming home,'' I offered.

''And Peter,'' Ruth said. She bit her thumbnail. ''I—I
wonder whether his parents have heard anything.''

''Why don't you telephone them?'' Papa suggested.

We all gasped. Papa never suggested long-distance calls.

''It is a special occasion,'' Papa explained.

''Oh, thank you, Papa!''

Ruth went to the telephone, which stood on a small table
in an alcove between the living room and dining room. There
was no door, no privacy. ''Operator, I'd like to place a long-
distance call to Michigan.'' A pause. ''Oh. Would you try
again?''

At last Ruth came back to the table, dejected. "Can't get a line out," she said. Then she added, "Peter's all right. I know it. I feel it."

"It might take a few months for all of them to get back," Mother said with a quick glance at Papa.

"I don't mind that," Ruth said. "I'll wait for years, as long as I know he's coming home."

She spoke with such passion that we all fell silent, almost embarrassed.

Lisa frowned and pushed back her hair. "Some soldiers might be sent out again," Lisa said. "To the Pacific. I heard a report about it on the radio."

"Stop it!" Ruth cried, clapping her hands over her ears. "I don't want to hear it. You! You have nothing to worry about. Your boyfriends are all draft dodgers."

"How can you say such a thing!" Lisa cried. "Nate's 4-F. He's got only one kidney! And he's doing defense work—how can you slander him?"

"Quiet!" Papa roared. He smacked his hand down on the table, hard. "I don't want to hear any of this."

I kept my eyes down on my plate. Something rose in me, a certain anguish, a question: Why? Why wouldn't we just be happy? And if not happy, at least peaceful together?

I thought of camp, and suddenly I felt overwhelmed with the desire for open spaces, trees, the beauty of mountains and lakes. I knew the timing was wrong, but I felt ready to burst.

"My counselor," I blurted out, "has picked me out for a wonderful opportunity." The moment I'd said it, I felt it was a brilliant strategy; if I had any chance at all, it was for Lisa and Ruth to come to my defense.

Everyone talked at once. "Annie is so smart."

"Did you win a prize?"

"She's being overdramatic, as usual."

"Let her talk!" shouted Lisa.

Stubbornly I kept my mouth shut tight and I shook my head. Let them pry it out of me!

"We're waiting, my dear child," Mother said. "Tell us."

"My counselor said I can go to summer camp in the mountains. It's a beautiful place."

"Camp?" Mother glanced about, as if seeking an interpreter. "They want to send you away? Why?"

"For fun," I said.

"Girls do go to camp, Mother," Lisa said.

"It would do her good, I think," added Ruth.

"Who is the father in this house?" Papa demanded. "Are you going to tell me that you—the three of you girls—are going to decide everything now? Who goes where?"

I closed my eyes. I felt tears starting. "Please, Papa," I whispered. "Just think about it."

Papa bit his lips together. From outside on the street we suddenly heard firecrackers going off, like New Year's Eve.

"We need you at home this summer," Papa began. "Who runs this camp? I need time to think about this. Do we have to decide tonight?"

"No," I said. "But pretty soon." I held my breath. Already, this was a small victory; Papa didn't usually think things over.

Papa nodded. "We'll see," he said. "Tonight, we will drink schnapps. It is a victory, after all."

Papa went to the sideboard and brought out a bottle of schnapps. He pried open the cork and took out five small liquor glasses of cut crystal. Solemnly he poured a small amount into each glass and passed them around. When he came to me, Mama seemed about to speak; Papa shook his head slightly and proceeded.

He lifted his glass. "To victory," he said. "To life." And he added the Hebrew equivalent, "*L'chaim.*"

"*L'chaim,*" we all said, and drank our schnapps. The sweet, strong liquor burned my throat and chest, a bittersweet burning, like our feelings now.

We did the dishes, all three of us, quickly and without arguments, for once. When we were finished, Ruth motioned to me.

"Come into my room," she said.

I was astonished. Ruth usually kept her room totally private.

Lisa shrugged and gave me a grin.

I went into Ruth's room. Once a sun porch, it was narrow and long, with a full row of windows looking out to the side yard. The flowered cotton bedspread matched the draw curtain Ruth had installed across the makeshift closet. On her wicker desk books, paper, and colored pencils were neatly aligned.

Ruth motioned me to sit down on the wicker chair; she hated to have anyone sit on her bed.

"I've got some stuff for you," she said, bending down over her bottom bureau drawer. She shook out a skirt, black-and-yellow plaid with wide pleats.

"Do you want this?" she asked.

"Want it?" I gasped. "I love it!"

"Take it," she said. She reached in once more, brought out a green, two-piece wool dress, with a long bodice on which was appliquéd a beautiful bird with red and golden patches. "You like this dress?"

"Like it! You know I do."

"You can have it," Ruth said.

I couldn't believe it. Ruth seldom gave anything away. I gave her a hug, and she endured it, then said, "Go on now, I have to do some work for tomorrow."

In my room I pulled off my jeans and tried on the green dress. I turned before the mirror, assessing my development. Just a few weeks before, I had bought my first bra, with Lisa's help. The dress somehow accentuated what was there and compensated for what wasn't. The dress was gorgeous. My hair shone very dark against the bright green fabric, and my skin seemed to glow.

Lisa came in, her hair wet from washing. She let out a whistle. "Wow," she said. "You look great."

"Really?" I turned from side to side.

"Better than those jeans," she said. "Why do you always dress like a boy? You're not a bad-looking girl, you know."

Lisa sat down at the dressing table and wound her hair into pin curls. Then she touched up her nail polish. When she was done, she held out her nails and blew on them lightly.

"Can you keep a secret?" she asked with a dazzling smile.

"Sure." I sat down on my bed, leaning toward her. I loved secrets.

"I've been invited to dance with a traveling show, all over the country. Madam Jacqueline called me today."

"Lisa! On the stage! On the stage!" I hugged myself to keep from squealing. "Can you? Would Papa let you?"

Lisa sat down on the bed beside me, her head close to

mine. "I don't even need to try out," she whispered excitedly. "They'd take me on her recommendation, because Madam is known as one of the best ballet teachers in Hollywood—actually, in the country."

"When would you leave? How long would you be away?" I muffled my voice with my hands. "Aren't you excited?"

She nodded, smiling mysteriously. "I have to let Madam know in July. It starts in August. I guess if they like me I'd stay awhile with the show, then try out for something better, maybe on Broadway."

I felt dizzy. Broadway! My sister on Broadway!

Then I realized what that meant. My eyes filled with tears. I wanted to beg her, "Don't go! Don't leave me."

But Lisa was waltzing around the room with a dreamy expression on her face. "It's not up to Papa," she whispered. "It's my decision, after all."

Mother called from the hall, sounding irritated. "Lisa, telephone. Tell your friends not to call so late."

Lisa waltzed out to the telephone, and I was left alone with Skippy. I pulled him close to me, under the covers. "I want to go to camp, Skippy," I whispered to him. "It doesn't mean that I don't love you."

3

Welcome to Quaker Pines

MY PARENTS WERE IN THE KITCHEN TALKING ABOUT ME.

"She was sick all February and March. She's not strong enough for all that activity."

"It's true, Arthur. She never knows her limits. Probably there will be boys at the camp."

"Roughnecks," said my father. "I see them on the street, acting like animals. And I don't know this Quaker church. What means inter-denom-inational?"

On and on it went; I heard their voices rumbling through the walls. Resentment almost boiled over inside me. What did they think I'd do at camp? Why couldn't they trust me?

"On the other hand," said my mother, "maybe she needs a change sometimes, like we all do."

"Why would she need a change? Don't we give her everything she needs?"

Mother replied softly, "She is growing up, Arthur. Maybe she needs other people."

Stiffly my father said, "She is very difficult sometimes. And with the baby coming . . . "

I froze, then ran out into the hall, ready to confront them. How could they have a baby at their age? Impossible. Ridiculous! But—a baby! I did want a little sister or brother.

"I haven't told Annie yet, about Daphne coming to stay here. It's only two weeks. . . ."

I leaned against the wall, disappointed and upset. Daphne was Dr. and Mrs. Belzac's baby, coming to stay while her parents went on vacation, probably. Mama wanted time alone with the baby. I knew it was silly to feel jealous. My mother loved babies the way I loved books and music and animals.

In the end it was like many small weights on a scale, all combining to change the balance. Papa found out from his friend, Harry Miles, that the Quaker church was respectful of other faiths. They would not try to convert me. Dr. Belzac told Mother I was certainly healthy enough to go to camp. But what really swayed the balance, I think, was that there was so much commotion at home that Mother was glad to get rid of me.

Ruth had a week off. She stormed through the house brooding about Peter, irritable and spoiling for a fight. Lisa was always expecting a phone call. Papa wanted the line kept clear for business. Lisa complained bitterly, "Why can't we get another telephone, like most civilized people?"

"Why don't you pay for it, instead of wasting all your money on cosmetics?" Ruth retorted.

"At least I contribute to the rent, which is more than you can say," Lisa shot back.

"All you think about is money. You're a regular gold digger, everyone says you are only going with Nate because he gives you gifts. You're getting a bad reputation. People talk about you. . . ."

"Only people with filthy minds," Lisa screamed. "Like you!"

I was in the kitchen with Mother, wiping the dishes. I'd heard a saying: Timing is everything. Into the ringing chaos I calmly asked, "Mother, may I go to summer camp?"

Mother dumped out the dishwater, wiped her hands, and knotted up the towel. "Yes," she said. "Go! Maybe," she added with a shudder, "you could arrange to take Lisa and Ruth with you!"

I don't know how she managed it with Papa. The next day, after school, he said to me, "I hear you are going to summer camp in the mountains."

I nodded. "Yes."

"And they have horses?"

"Yes, and maybe other animals, too," I said.

"I like animals," Papa said. "Marvelous, when you think about it, how each animal exists in its own way. When I was a boy," he went on, "I never had an animal. My parents didn't believe in it."

"Why not, Papa?" I asked. Papa seldom talked about his childhood.

He shrugged. "Who knows?"

That was the strange thing about Papa; he never asked why about things, the way I did.

"I'll need some clothes for camp," I said.

"What kind of clothes?" he asked, staring at me.

"Another pair of jeans," I said. "And T-shirts and flannel shirts. It gets cold in the mountains at night. And I'll need a jacket."

"Where do you buy all these things?" Papa asked. He put his hand in his pocket, as if to hold on to his change.

"I thought I'd go with Marjorie to the army-navy surplus store. They have peacoats and stuff. I also need a canteen. For hikes."

"How do expect to pay for all this?" Papa asked.

"I—maybe I could earn some money." Nervously I licked my lips, felt my eyes stinging. "I could sew for you, and maybe do some more baby-sitting."

Mrs. Schatz next door had asked me to baby-sit a few times. I tried to calculate how many hours of baby-sitting, at thirty cents an hour, it would take to equal all the camp clothes I needed.

"Well, your birthday is coming up," Papa said. "Maybe I could give you money for your birthday this year ahead of time."

"That would be great!" I exclaimed. Then, needing to be practical, I asked, "How much money?"

"Twenty dollars," Papa promptly answered. "You are going to be thirteen, no?

"Yes."

"A teenager. That is a big birthday. A teenage girl is a young lady already."

With my savings and Papa's twenty dollars I managed to buy a jacket, boots, a pair of jeans, four shirts, two flannel and two cotton, and a canteen. Marjorie and I spent an entire Saturday and two afternoons shopping. It was glorious.

I laid everything out on the bed to show Lisa that night. I tried on the heavy hiking shoes I'd gotten at the surplus store for three dollars and a quarter.

Lisa laughed at the shoes. "Not very feminine," she said.

"I don't care," I retorted. "I wish we could all go camping and cook out and sleep in a tent. Don't you?"

"Hardly," Lisa said with a smirk. "What about bugs? Bears?" She shuddered. "Who wants to sleep on the ground?"

"You can see the stars," I said.

Lisa gave me a quick, tender look. "Quite so," she said softly. She regarded me from head to toe and asked, "What are you going to do for a bathing suit?"

"I'll take my old one," I said.

"Not on your life," Lisa objected. "It's too small. And it's way stretched out in back." Suddenly she launched into one of her favorite imitations, Mammy from *Gone with the Wind*. "It ain't fittin', chile, yo fanny stickin' way out jes' lak a hussy—ain't fittin'!"

I sank down on the bed, laughing; then I quickly became sober. "I don't have any more money for a bathing suit. I guess—I don't know. Maybe I won't swim. But then I'll look weird. Oh, Lisa, I don't know. Maybe I shouldn't even go to camp."

"Don't be stupid," Lisa snapped. She stood before me, her hands on her hips. "I was planning to buy you a bathing suit for your birthday," she said. "They're having a sale at the Eastern Columbia. I thought we'd go down there Saturday—unless you mind getting your present ahead of time."

"Oh, Lisa!"

I hugged her so hard that I knocked her over, and then we were both on the bed, laughing and tickling and wrestling, and Lisa held me off, launching into an imitation of James

Cagney, "Listen, sweetheart, if you think you're going to put the hooks on me . . ."

I ached with laughter.

Mother walked by, shaking her head. "You two," she said, but she was beaming.

Ah, I thought, sometimes life is almost too good to bear!

Marjorie left first. Her parents took me to the train station with them to say good-bye.

Marjorie and I hugged and kissed and cried. "Write everything in your journal, Annie, and I'll do the same, and we'll compare when we see each other. Oh, I'm going to miss you so much!"

"Good-bye, have a great summer," I called, and waved until the train puffed away.

Three days later it was time for me to leave. The pickup point was at the Sears Roebuck parking lot just a few miles from my house. Two old buses, marked CHARTER, stood in the parking lot, dwarfed by the vast expanse of empty cement and the sky, filled with puffy clouds, all tinged with the first light of the morning sun.

"Why do they have to leave so early?" Mother asked.

"It's a pretty long bus ride," I said. The buses would take us to the town of San Jacinto, Miss Broderick had told me. From there, we would go up the mountain by truck.

We were early. As we stood there waiting, I shivered slightly, wishing for a familiar face. Cars pulled up, kids climbed out, some calling to one another, old friends from past summers. I felt alone and strange. I didn't know anyone.

"Where are these children from?" Mother asked in a low voice. Papa was taking my bags out of the car.

"All over L.A., I guess," I replied, keeping my face blank and looking straight ahead. I knew the reason for Mother's question; the boys and girls that now began to cluster in groups, talking and laughing, were like those we had left behind when we moved farther to the west of the city a few years ago. There were black kids, Mexican kids, a few Chinese. It was an international gathering. We should have felt right at home. I felt nervous and tense.

I saw Papa give Mama a cautionary glance as he came over to us. He had a strange expression on his face, doubt combined with interest. Papa was always interested in new people. He told me once, after our Japanese neighbors had been taken away to the relocation camps, he was sorry he had never met the father. "He would have had something to say," was Papa's way of explaining it. He had shaken his head and seemed sorry, almost guilty, about the quick departure of the Japanese. Other times, he had cursed them all for bombing Pearl Harbor and prolonging the war.

Now Papa carried my duffel bag over to the bus, and I carried the sleeping bag I'd borrowed from Marjorie. It belonged to her brother. Mother had rolled an extra blanket inside it, and she had also bought me two rolls of Life Savers for the trip.

As we stood and watched the buses being loaded, Papa handed me three folded dollar bills. "Here," he said. "Put this in your pocket. Maybe you'll need money for stamps."

"Mama gave me twelve envelopes, already stamped," I said.

Papa smiled, then lit a cigarette and tossed the match away. "Maybe you will find another way to spend it," he said. "I never sat on a horse," he added thoughtfully. "Never in my life. So"—he shrugged—"maybe you will tell me how it is."

Mama fussed over me and worried. I saw the other parents, hands in pockets, talking to each other and making jokes; nobody else seemed to be full of fear as my mother was. "Don't swim unless there is a counselor with you," she reminded me. "If you go on a hike, keep with the group. Don't go out into the forest alone, do you hear me?"

"Yes, yes," I said, and nodded to everything, wishing only to be away from Mama's fretful voice and those bleak warnings.

But when the buses were loaded and we campers were called aboard, I had this terrible lump in my throat. I waved and mouthed the words, "I love you, Mama!" My parents waved back and smiled at me, and then, to my great joy, I saw that they were talking to other parents, and Papa was laughing with another man.

In the bus a few boys were yelling and punching each other. A counselor named Ty made them settle down. Kids were saving seats for one another; everyone seemed to have a friend or a sister or brother along, except me. I sat next to the window, with nobody beside me.

Last night Lisa and I had lain awake, talking. She told me about the camp she went to in Maine, when we first came to America.

"It was a beautiful place," she whispered, "with a lake and boats and tennis courts. Most of the girls had their own tennis rackets and cute little tennis dresses, and they brought lots of spending money. I was the charity case," she said.

"Quaker Pines isn't like that," I said stoutly, though I

wasn't at all sure. Miss Broderick had recommended me; my parents only had to pay for bus transportation. Maybe I was a "charity case," too.

The bus creaked, groaned, and began to move, and as it rumbled along the streets, I felt dizzy with apprehension, and wished I was home again in my own bed, with Skippy lying against my feet.

I glanced at the girl across the aisle. The boy beside her was obviously her little brother. Her skin was smooth and dark, her lips full. I glanced again at her hair, wound into several small, tight braids, and I noticed the little gold hoop earrings she wore. I'd have given anything to wear gold earrings like those.

In kindergarten and first grade I'd had a black girlfriend, Janet. I used to love the way she talked and moved. I admired her dark, gleaming skin, and her mom made the best potato turnovers I'd ever eaten in my life. Janet moved away, though, and as we got older, kids didn't mingle the same way. Junior high, in fact, was broken into territories, as inviolate as if they'd been fenced off. All the black kids ate together behind the gym, except for the athletes, and they sat on the side lawn. Oh, we talked to each other, saying polite hellos or giving each other the assignments. We didn't fight, nor did we socialize. It was as if an invisible shield kept us separated.

I leaned toward the girl across the aisle and smiled. "Hi," I said hopefully. "My name's Annie. What's yours?"

Her name was Tallahassee Davis, Tally for short, and I loved the way she laughed and talked, with quick gestures and a wide smile. I shared my Life Savers with Tally and her little brother, Herbie. We talked and told jokes and joined the others in some songs. At last the bus stopped at the foot of the mountains and we all got out. I was dazed from the long ride. My stomach felt queasy.

"You'll be sick before we get up the mountain," Tally told me, "unless you want to suck on these here lemons." Tallahassee produced a small brown sack which contained several lemons, cut into wedges, wrapped in waxed paper. "Keeps you from getting car sick," she said. "Don't eat too much, either. I'll hang on to the lemons and you just ask me when you want some."

I smiled my thanks. "I guess you've been to Quaker Pines before," I said.

"Twice," said Tally with a vigorous nod. "Herbie's never been, though. He just turned eight." She smiled at her brother, then yanked him close to her, saying sternly, "You stay where I can watch you, hear?"

"I have to go to the bathroom," Herbie whispered.

"Okay, then, I'll take you," said Tallahassee, throwing me a knowing look, and I was astonished to see her heading straight for the door that said WOMEN, with her little brother in tow. Apparently Tallahassee had her own way of doing things.

Kids hung around eating oranges they had brought. I felt stupid for not thinking of it. Mother had offered to pack me a lunch. I had refused, imagining people would think it weird. Now, of course, I was sorry as the other kids brought out their sandwiches. Some went into the roadside snack shack and came out with hot dogs and fries.

"They're gonna cough it all up," said Tally as she joined me again, grinning. "All that grease. If you're hungry, just get a Coke," she advised, "or eat an orange."

I dug into my pocket and brought out one of the dollars Papa had given me. Tallahassee and I stood in line at the little window with a bunch of other kids. Some of them knew Tallahassee and said, "Hey, how're you? You bring your brother?"

I noticed how there were no territories here; kids talked and joked—white, black, Mexican, whatever. They walked with their arms around each other.

One boy, older than we were, obviously on the staff, wore a khaki shirt with several hiking pins on the pocket. His hair and clothes looked so fresh that he might have dropped here, suddenly, by parachute. The rest of us looked wrinkled and weary. Not this guy.

"Hey, Tally, how's it going?" he called out, and his smile lit up the universe. A wide smile, without any hesitation, it said that life was good, that we were lucky people just to be here. Seeing him, I believed it.

"Great, John. It's been a good year. I brought my little brother. This here's Herbie."

"Hey, Herbie! Put her there!" John thrust out his hand to greet the little boy, and Herbie's face shone. "I'll bet you are a good baseball player, I can see by those muscles."

"I guess so," said Herbie, modestly repressing a grin.

"Soon as we get to camp, let's hit a few," offered John. He turned to me and nodded. "Hi. I'm John Wright."

"Annie," I said, without thinking; I should have said Ann, which seemed to me much more grown up.

"Annie Laurie," John said with a big smile. "Like the song. You know it?"

"Sure," I said. It was a favorite of mine.

"Maxwellton's braes are bonnie,
Where early falls the dew.
'Twas there that Annie Laurie
Gave me her promise true.
Gave me her promise true,
Which ne'er forgot will be. . . ."

He started to hum the song, then to sing it. I felt my cheeks flaming. I'd never had anyone sing to me before.

John stopped and told us, "My mom is Scottish. My dad's part Irish. We all go really soft for those old ballads."

Tally smiled, and I'd have changed my name to Annie Laurie at that very moment if I could. I'd have changed myself to that lassie who gave her promise true, especially if the promise was to someone like John.

"Are you a counselor?" I asked him.

"Yeah. Not entirely full-fledged yet. But I'm working on it. You have to be eighteen," he added.

So he was sixteen, or maybe even seventeen. I was awed. I'd never even talked to a high school boy before, except for the boys who dated my sisters, and that was entirely different.

John nodded toward my Coke. "Smart girl," he said. "It's not good to eat much before we take the trucks."

I smiled. "Sounds like a roller coaster," I remarked.

"You like roller coasters?" John asked. He leaned toward me, waiting for an answer, as if it really mattered.

"I've never been on one," I admitted. "I do love the Ferris wheel, though."

"That's my favorite," said John. "I like to reach up and touch the sky. Once, I grabbed me a star," he said, and laughed.

Tally and Herbie and I laughed as if this was the cleverest, funniest thing we had ever heard.

Tally knew why. As we walked back to the bus she bent toward me and whispered, "Gotcha, didn't he?"

I didn't know what to say.

"All the girls are crazy about John Wright," she said. "And he makes 'em all feel like the cat's meow, that's for sure."

We climbed up into the back of a large truck, its panel sides swaying against the weight of the kids propped against them. Some stood. Some sat down on the floor of the truck.

"Better stand," Tallahassee told me. "Hang over the edge. That way you don't lose your balance." She held on to Herbie.

Soon enough I understood Tallahassee's warning. As the truck strained up the mountains, the back end of it lurched wildly from side to side, flinging campers to the left, then to the right, a mass movement of bodies accompanied by groans, shouts, squeals.

I braced myself, felt my head spinning and my stomach aching. The experienced campers leaned into the turns, and they sang out a chorus of whooping sounds each time the direction changed: "Whoo! Whoo! Whoo!"

I felt a sudden rush of panic, as if I were to be suffocated by these sounds and all these swaying bodies. Images flashed past me—trains, black skies, nights of terror, sounds of sirens . . . I reached out to Tallahassee. Wordlessly she handed me a lemon wedge, and she nodded encouragement as I began to suck.

Miraculously, the nausea passed. With it, my fear also evaporated, and I found myself suddenly invigorated, excited to have emerged on the other side of panic. Now as the other kids hollered and whooped their approval of the wild ride, I joined them, laughing and yelling, yelling with nobody to care or to try to stop me. I lifted my head, leaned over the side of the truck and felt my hair flying, my eyes blurred from speed and dust and sheer exhilaration.

Turning back, I saw John Wright looking at me, grinning. " 'Atta girl!" he yelled. " 'Atta girl!" and he nodded his approval.

At long last the truck slowed and then veered into a series of deep ruts, and the veteran campers, who knew this was the last lap, began to cheer and sing:

"Quaker Pines, oh, how we love,
Blue skies above,
Your fragrant trees,
And buzzing bees,
The lake so cold,
And mountains bold,
But ever in our memory
Are all the campers pledged to thee.
None finer than
A Quaker Piner
Ever, ever will be."

One last terrific bump, and we landed and rushed out of the truck and looked around. In that moment I took it all in—

the smell of the pine trees, the great, green mountains beyond, the boulders upon the hill, the little log cabins, and, in the distance, the twinkling edges of the lake, silvery in the sunlight. I breathed deeply, and I knew I had come to a new world.

Another truck, containing our luggage and a few stragglers, came driving up, dust billowing all around it, meeting the dust under our feet. Out popped a tall and lanky man, who was greeted by cheers from the old campers and quickly introduced to all of us as Ed. Handyman, shopper, delivery boy, Ed would take any requests of ours to the village, where he went nearly every morning to purchase necessities for the camp and for individual campers.

"That doesn't include candy bars or gum," called out Douglas, the camp director, and everybody laughed.

With Ed came three other counselors, one a redheaded girl of about seventeen, named Ellen. She was absolutely beautiful: tall and poised, with long, shining hair, large brown eyes, and a brilliant smile.

Apparently she was a favorite among the returning campers, for in moments Ellen was surrounded by kids hugging her arms, yelling for her attention, pushing to get near her.

I saw John Wright watching her, saw on his face a look of admiration, almost awe. I felt a twisting sensation in my middle. Envy, the old enemy, had followed me even here. I knew that feeling, when Lisa and Ruth got phone calls and dates and went to parties, and I had to stay home.

"Call me when you're sixteen!" my sisters' boyfriends would say, and sometimes they even flipped a nickel at me, and I'd be mortified.

Now Douglas pointed out the cabins and the lodge.

Unaccountably, I felt a blurring. I began to shiver. I couldn't stop. I still smelled the pines and heard the birds and the chattering of squirrels. Everything seemed exquisitely clear, except for my own body, which was turning numb, beginning with my lips, then my cheeks, then my fingers.

Oh, God! God! I silently cried, don't let me be sick please! Not here!

I was able to stay up long enough to meet my assigned cabin mates, Tallahassee and three other girls named Becca, Lenore, and Nancy Rae.

I briefly glanced at each of them. Becca was a small brunet with her hair bobbed and a bright smile. Lenore wore glasses; she seemed gentle and nice. Then there was Nancy Rae. With gray eyes, her light hair done in a single braid, thin nose, and wide, freckled face, Nancy Rae looked tough as steel.

A feeling, tight around the throat, seemed to grab me. Something about Nancy Rae was familiar and sickening. Can faces really reveal what's within? I thought so, or else why would I immediately have felt such dislike? She sized me up, too, and narrowed her eyes and lifted her head, looking superior.

Nancy Rae hoisted her large bag up onto her shoulder. "Hey, guys!" she bellowed, taking charge, "let's race. Last one in the cabin is a rotten egg!"

I struggled with my heavy bag, and I managed at last to get it up the steps of our cabin. The next thing I knew, I blacked out. Of course, I was the rotten egg.

4

Mary the Angel

IT WAS ALMOST LIKE COMING OUT OF THE ANESTHETIC WHEN I'd had my appendix removed.

Outside it was dark. I had the haunted feeling of having awakened to another time, another century, perhaps. I thought of my family, each one. Their faces chastened me, as if they were saying, "Well, *you* wanted to leave. Now you're alone." A rush of homesickness overwhelmed me. I lay on my side, quietly crying, when suddenly I heard a sound in the branches, *whoo-ooo*, *krhoo-ooo*.

An owl!

Propped up on one elbow, I looked around and saw that this was a large, one-room log house, larger than the other cabins, with a brightly colored rag rug on the floor, and five beds in a row against the back wall. The larger part of the room contained a desk, a washbasin, several chairs, and shelves into which were stuffed what appeared like hundreds of games.

Here . . . home . . . I felt torn between two poles. Somehow I wondered whether home was still there. Did they miss me? Did they care?

From outside I heard voices. The campers were singing. Their voices echoed over the entire camp, and suddenly I longed to be in the center of things, among them. But I felt tired, so very tired and weak.

Now I could make out the words to the song:

"No man is an island
No man stands alone,
Each man's joy is joy to me,
Each man's grief is my own. . . ."

No man stands alone . . . how lovely, I thought. How wonderful that would be, if we were all connected.

"Hello there!" came a voice, and I now saw the woman sitting at a small desk; she was round faced, with long, straight, dark hair hanging down her back. "You look much better. Do you know what happened?"

"No. I guess I fainted."

She laughed. "You certainly did. I'm Beatrice, the camp nurse. You must have been exhausted, child."

The word, *child*, suddenly brought tears to my eyes. When had I gotten so tired? It seemed as if I had never been well, and memories of lying in bed sick mounted up, crowding out everything else.

"Now, now, it's frightening to faint, isn't it," Beatrice said cheerfully. "Have you been away from home before?"

"No," I said. Then quickly I added, "Well, when we were in Switzerland, I had to go to this camp because I was sick. . . ."

"Ah," said Beatrice with a nod and a smile. "You were probably very little, and you needed your mama. Now you're a young lady, and I'm sure by tomorrow you'll be right as rain."

I tried a smile. "Don't say rain," I murmured.

"That's the spirit!" Beatrice said with an encouraging smile. "We'll hope for sunshine. Bet we'll get it, too. Do you like swimming? The lake is wonderful."

"I love to swim," I said. "But I'm not very good."

"That's what you came for, isn't it? To learn new skills?"

"Yes, I guess so." New skills. I perked up at the idea of getting new skills—I certainly needed them, I thought.

"There's so much to learn here," Beatrice went on. "We're going to do some nature hikes, learn Indian lore, like tracking and marking trails. I'm Indian—three-quarter Navaho, one-quarter Cherokee."

Before I could digest this astonishing news, I heard a voice from the doorway. "Dinnertime!"

There stood a slim, blond woman holding a tray in her hands, with a small girl beside her. I was startled to see her; something about her seemed very familiar—an air of quiet authority, a way of walking that made her seem, rather, to glide.

Beatrice jumped up and took the tray from her, saying, "Mary, how nice of you—I would have gotten it."

"Nonsense, you go on and get your supper in the lodge, Beatrice. I'll sit with our patient for a while."

The woman strode toward me, more serious than smiling, holding her little girl by the hand. Mary wore pale beige riding pants, a soft blue flannel shirt, and sensible boots. She smiled warmly and said, "Hello, Annie, I'm Mary, the codirector. Sorry you weren't feeling well. But you look much better now."

"She'll be fine," said Beatrice.

"Of course she will." Mary pulled up the straw-bottomed chair and sat down, and the little girl laid her head in her mother's lap. The child was adorable, about three, a replica of her mother, with delicate skin, full lips, and a long, gentle face.

"Alice," said her mother, "this is Annie; say hello."

"Hi, Alice," I said. I patted the bed with its puffy quilt. "Want to sit up here with me?"

Wordlessly, Alice shook her head, but she immediately climbed up beside me. I put my arm around her; her hair smelled slightly like lemon and flowers. I had always wanted a little sister.

"We have kittens," Alice said solemnly.

"You do?" I exclaimed. "I adore kittens, almost more than anything."

"Then you must visit the barn," Mary said. "We have a small menagerie."

I wasn't certain of the word *menagerie*, but I nodded, unwilling to show my ignorance.

"I've brought you a book," Mary said, sliding the volume out from under her arm. "*A Girl of the Limberlost*. It's always been a favorite of mine."

"Mine, too," I exclaimed. "I love that book. I've read it three or four times."

"Oh." Mary smiled. "Well, there are plenty of other books here, I just thought . . . "

"I'll read it again," I said. "I read all my favorites over and over."

"A girl after my own heart," said Mary, nodding and

laughing. "What good is a book if you read it only once? It's like having a favorite dress and leaving it in the closet after one wearing."

Mary moved the small table nearer to the bed. I swung my legs out and began to eat.

"This smells delicious," I said. There was a meat patty, salad, green beans, mashed potatoes, and banana cake. I realized that I hadn't eaten all day, and I ate eagerly, all except for the beans, which I moved to the edge of the plate.

"You don't like beans," Mary stated.

I tensed. I had been at places where we were forced to eat whatever we were given, no matter how repulsive.

"No," I said. "Must I eat them?"

"Of course not. In the lodge we serve family style. You help yourself to whatever you like. I don't think food is to be used as a punishment, do you?"

I laughed. It seemed so absurd, and Mary was so lovely.

I felt my strength returning, and I felt bold enough to ask Mary, "What was wrong with me? Why did I faint?"

Mary shrugged. "My best guess is you probably didn't get much sleep last night, and with the heat and that truck ride—it happens. And maybe it's your monthly time. At the beginning, that can get your system all haywire, too."

I nodded. Though Mary was a stranger, I didn't feel embarrassed, any more than I'd be with my sister. I looked at her lovely eyes and her gentle, intelligent face, and I wanted more than anything in the world to be her friend.

I told her about my pets, the rabbits I once had, and the duck, the many cats, and Skippy, especially Skippy.

"Does Skippy do tricks?" Alice asked.

"Oh, yes," I said. "I've taught him to walk a plank, as if it was a tightrope. And he begs and rolls over, and sometimes we play hide-and-seek."

"Oh, I love that dog!" squealed Alice, hugging herself.

"Do you like horses?" Mary asked.

"Oh, yes," I quickly said. "Although, I've never known any personally. I've read a lot of stories about horses."

"You'll have to meet my mare, Molly," she said. "As soon as you're feeling better."

I realized I was feeling better—not only better, but terrific.

Alice tapped me on the arm and asked, "Do you know how to play fish?"

"Sure," I said. "I love to play fish. Want to play with me tomorrow?"

"All right," said Alice. "I'll come in the morning and get into your bed."

"You'll do no such thing," Mary said, laughing.

We talked about books and about horses, and the time passed so quickly that I was startled when Beatrice returned, and sorry to see Mary and Alice walking toward the door. Too soon they were gone, and I lay back, thumbing through the novel Mary had brought me, and with a start I realized what had seemed so oddly familiar. The Angel—yes, Elnora's friend and helper, the Angel in the story; somehow Mary reminded me, from that very first moment, of her.

Beatrice bustled about, tidying things. She pointed to a door. "You can use this lavatory tonight," she said. "Tomorrow, it's the outhouse, like everyone else."

"Outhouse?" I repeated. "You're kidding," I said.

Beatrice shook her head and grinned. "That's camping," she said cheerfully. "Might as well get used to it."

I went and got my jeans from the chair. "I might as well start getting used to it right now," I said firmly, pulling on my jeans and my shoes. "I don't really need to stay in here."

"But . . . are you sure? You can sleep here tonight, if you want. I sleep here, too." Beatrice pointed to a bed near the sink.

"No. Really. I feel fine."

"Annie, you did pass out," said Beatrice. "Kids sometimes pretend to be sick just because they want to sleep in these beds and use the indoor plumbing. But you don't have to try to prove anything."

I said, "I just want to go to my cabin with my friends."

I remembered how nice it had been talking to Tally on the bus, and now I recalled meeting the other girls, Becca, Lenore, and Nancy Rae. I also remembered Nancy Rae's challenge, and the way she had glanced at me with a look of disgust or even hatred. Could I have imagined it?

I put on my jacket and stepped out into the night. Cold air hit me like a hand. The frost from my breath stood white before my face. I looked up at the sky, deep black and filled with stars. Never had I seen so many stars. They shone like bright crystals, sweeping across the sky. The same stars here, I thought, as at home.

I realized, for the first time, that I was a little afraid of the dark, of the thought of hands darting out to grab me, and spooky things in the night.

Nonsense, I told myself, imagining Mary's voice. Go on up the road to the little hut—*go on*!

Slowly I picked my way around the infirmary, then up a small hill behind the building, where the outhouse stood.

As I approached, an astonishing odor accosted me. Whatever I had imagined about camping, this wasn't part of it. I was used to city things, proper sinks and toilets—not outhouses or a mere faucet and a pan for washing.

To make matters worse, the outhouse accommodated three; it was already occupied by two other girls who, when I knocked, yelled out, laughing, "Come in! The more the merrier!"

What about privacy? I felt choked up with embarrassment and dread. But I opened the door and went in, holding my breath and giving myself encouragement; it's normal and natural, nothing to be ashamed of. This is camping. This is camp life. Oh, God!

I settled myself alongside the other two girls. "Hi," I said weakly. "My name's Annie Platt."

They introduced themselves, Sandra and Brittany. They were both in the cabin just beyond mine.

Suddenly a roll of toilet paper whizzed past my head. I reached out, caught it, sent it flying down to the girl on the end. It sailed back. "Hot potato! Hot potato!" we giggled, tossing the paper roll back and forth.

"What a place to meet!" Sandra shrieked.

"Whew! It stinks so bad in here!" laughed Brittany.

I said, "Glad I'm not alone, though. This place would be real spooky in the middle of the night!"

"I'd *never* go here alone in the middle of the night, *never*," said Brittany.

"Me, neither," I readily agreed.

"Hey, we've got flashlights," Sandra said. "We'll light your way back."

They guided me back with their flashlights and I made my way up the path to cabin seven. I felt initiated, tough and competent. I thought of Lisa, how she would shrink back at the very idea of using an outhouse, especially without privacy. Privacy was a big thing in my family, I realized. I laughed aloud, remembering the toilet paper game; wouldn't Lisa just die!

I went up the path to cabin seven, pushed open the door, and stood, letting my eyes adjust to the darkness. I heard muffled laughter, then voices.

"Did you see those jeans?"

"She looks so weird."

"I think she's sort of cute."

"She's a sickie. I hate sickies." I recognized Nancy Rae's voice. There was no mistaking that coldness.

"I sort of feel sorry for her." This came from Becca.

"What's with you? You like to play nurse or something? It's going to be a drag, having her on hikes. . . . I'll bet she can't even swim or anything."

My heart thumped too hard in my chest. The cabin floor creaked under my footsteps. Nancy Rae yelled out, "Who is it? Who is it?"

Someone shone a flashlight straight into my eyes.

"Oh, it's you."

Behind the flashlight I could make out Nancy Rae, clad in red pajamas, and Becca beside her, pushing her sleek, dark hair away from her face, looking embarrassed.

"Hi, Annie," Becca said. "Are you better?"

I replied, "Yes, thanks. Where's Lenore and Tally?"

Becca shone the light onto the third bed: Lenore was sound asleep.

"Well," said Nancy Rae, "I sure hope you don't have anything catching."

"Maybe *you* have something catching," I said heatedly. "I just fainted. That's not catching." I felt like pinching those fat, freckled cheeks of hers.

"Well, since you're so tough," said Nancy Rae, "how about racing me across the lake tomorrow?"

"Fine by me," I said with a careless shrug, as if I was used to swimming across a lake any day of the year. There's only one way to treat kids like Nancy Rae, I thought; if they're mean, you have to be meaner. If they're tough, you have to be tougher. I'd had plenty of fights on the school yard—well, at least three, and I stood my ground each time.

From the other side of the cabin Tally came toward us, wearing a long white nightshirt. "Annie!" She smiled. "I guess I fell asleep. I'm so glad you're back!"

Tallahassee took my arm. "I got the two beds in the alcove for us. I put your stuff away in the shelf, is that okay?"

"Sure," I said. "Thanks."

"And I laid out your sleeping bag on the bed."

I got into my pajamas and burrowed down inside my sleeping bag.

"Nancy Rae's been telling us stories," Tally whispered. "About how she and her older brother hopped a train and rode it clear to Salinas, in the boxcar."

"Oh," I said, not wanting to call Nancy Rae a liar, but feeling very suspicious.

"She says by her house there's this big old deep canyon, and they have this big tree with a rope tied to it, and Nancy Rae says she can swing clear across to the other side and jump off."

"Good for Nancy Rae," I said. Then, yawning, I said, "Good night."

But I couldn't sleep yet. Me and my big mouth. I should race Nancy Rae across the lake? I just barely knew how to swim. Lisa had taught me the sidestroke and the crawl a few years ago. Trouble was, we hardly ever got to go swimming, maybe only twice each summer. We'd ride the bus down Wilshire Boulevard, almost all the way downtown to the Ambassador Hotel. It was a fabulous place, with a green canopy out front, and a doorman and all kinds of fancy-looking people. In back they had a huge patio, and a wide sandy area with sand brought all the way from the beach miles away, and of course, the most important part was the swimming pool.

About twice a year Lisa and I went there. The last two years we'd gone for my birthday. We'd have lunch at one of the tables, sitting under a striped umbrella. Afterward, we'd swim in the pool. I learned to swim across and back again, without stopping.

But the lake, I realized with a heavy feeling, the lake would be far different. The lake would be cold and deep and large, very large.

Maybe by tomorrow, I told myself, Nancy Rae would forget all about it. Maybe she didn't want to race any more than I did. For all I knew, maybe she couldn't even swim.

Of course, I thought logically, I could just say I didn't mean it. Take it back. Say I wasn't feeling well. Make up some excuse.

Oh, I could just hear Nancy Rae's taunts. "Chicken! Sickie!"

She had started it; I'd have to finish it now.

5

Nancy Rae Strikes Again -and Again

FIRST THING THE NEXT MORNING, I JUMPED OUT OF BED, teeth chattering, and ran to the outhouse. It was freezing. I had never been in the mountains before, never got up to that early-morning bite in the air, and the white haze of my own breath. Dew dripped down from the dark green pine needles. The ground seemed hard, frozen. The world here was cold and silent, almost spellbound, as if it were waiting. I felt that my life, so far, had been spent in small rooms and crowded spaces—here I could breathe.

Girls straggled out of their cabins, laughing, clattering the metal washbasins that we had to fill from the outdoor spigot, then set back onto homemade wooden frames; there were no real sinks.

I waited my turn, filled a basin from the tap, and quickly washed my hands and face. My teeth chattered from the freezing water, but I felt my entire body waking up.

"Hi, Annie!" Lenore came running up beside me, rubbing her hands together. "Is this your first year?"

I nodded.

"Mine, too," she said. "I don't know anybody."

"You know me," I said, smiling. "By tonight you'll probably know everybody."

Other girls, including Tallahassee, came into line; soon we were all talking, laughing, comparing schools, hometowns, families. I was filled with excitement; all those new friends! I wondered where the boys were, and I finally asked someone. All the girls laughed. "They keep 'em on the other side of the lake," someone said. "We all get together for meals and activities, though."

"Anyone special you're interested in?" asked Tally, as if she didn't know. The girls all started talking about the boys. It felt just like home. I thought of Marjorie, all the things I'd have to tell her. And I was happy to realize I didn't miss her, I didn't miss anybody! I was just excited to be here at Quaker Pines.

Back in our cabin, Nancy Rae and Becca were still burrowed into their sleeping bags.

"Hey! Get up!" called Lenore, Tally, and I.

"Go 'way," Becca grumbled. "It's freezing in here!"

"Get up," Tally teased, "or we'll have to give you the cold water treatment."

Tally began to count. "One. Two. Three." She turned to Lenore, laughing, and said, "You go get some water in your canteen, and we'll . . ."

"Come on," I cried, joining the game, tugging at Nancy Rae's sleeping bag. "You'll get used to it—it's only a shock for a minute. And that cold water outside—it actually feels good!"

Becca poked her arms out, reaching for her sweatshirt and pulling it on. "Whew!" she breathed. "This is *wild*!"

But Nancy Rae sat up and stared at me, her eyes narrowed menacingly. "Get your dirty hands off my sleeping bag," she said. "I don't like people to touch my stuff."

The others all turned in surprise at Nancy Rae. I saw the glint in her gray eyes; she looked ready to spring at me.

Tally rushed to my defense. "Why you picking on Annie? She never did anything to you."

Nancy Rae climbed out of bed. "Only kidding," she said, and looking directly at me, added, "I didn't mean anything, Annie. Can't you take a joke?"

"Sure," I muttered. But I still felt her coldness, worse than the temperature of the mountain morning.

"Don't mind her, Annie," Tallahassee murmured to me as we walked over to the lodge. Inside a fire was blazing in the hearth. It sent a wonderful aroma of pine wood throughout the room. I wondered why somebody is always along to spoil things.

"I can't stand her," I muttered.

Tally nodded. "I know."

We stood warming our hands, and Tally explained. "After today we'll have KP charts. We all take turns serving and clearing. Some sweep up and set tables for the next meal."

"Sounds like home," I said grimly.

Tallahassee giggled. "Ain't that the truth! Only, at home I get to cook and clean and do all the shopping besides."

"What about your mom?" I asked.

"What mom?" Tally gave me a look of exaggerated surprise. "My mom's long gone. Haven't seen her since I was two, and then, don't remember much."

"But your brother . . ."

"My daddy's had himself three different wives. Herbie's my brother from the second one. Then there's Delwina and Derrick from the third one. She's still with us." Tallahassee giggled. "Won't be for long, though. They're always fighting, her and my dad."

"Is she mean?" I asked, thinking of the stories about stepmothers.

"Not around enough to be mean," Tally said. "Mostly, she's fixing herself up ready to go out. She leaves me alone, so what do I care?" Tally shrugged.

"Where does she go?" I asked. "What does she do?"

"Day work," Tally said with a smirk.

That meant cleaning houses. "My mom used to do that," I told Tallahassee. "Before she got this job taking care of a baby."

"She did?" Tallahassee's look showed she thought I was joking—or fibbing, just to be nice.

"Yes. Really. I went with her sometimes. She worked for some rich ladies, cleaning house. She needed to. We were broke."

"Lots of white folks got broke in the depression," said Tallahassee gravely.

"We came from the war," I said. "From Germany. We had to leave all our money there."

Tally nodded and whistled out her breath in a long, low sound. "You were in the war?"

"Well, yes," I admitted. "Sort of."

"Did you see Hitler?"

"Once," I said, with a shiver. "I heard him. He was giving a speech in the big public square in Berlin. My mother said we had to stay and listen."

"How come?"

"If the Nazis saw us leaving, they'd know we were against him. They'd know we were Jews. So . . ."

Tally wrinkled her brow, nodding deeply. "That was bad times," she said sympathetically.

"Yes," I said. I wanted to forget. I knew I never would. "But it's over now," I said. "At least the Nazis are defeated."

"My dad says we ought to bomb them to kingdom come. My dad works in a defense plant. He's a welder," she said proudly. "Sometimes he works nights, sometimes days. It makes my stepmom crazy! My dad works real hard," she added soberly. Suddenly she laughed. "Hey! Let's go get ourselves some breakfast! I smell eggs, bacon, hotcakes— oh, man!"

Eggs, bacon, hotcakes, oh, man! sang in my mind as the breakfast gong now sounded and we crowded into the lodge with the other kids.

When the bell stopped sounding, Mary, with Alice on her arm, called out, "Sit in your cabin groups, please. Today the oldest and the youngest at each table will get the serving trays. After that, we'll follow the KP charts."

Apparently it was tradition for the boys to sit on the right side of the room and the girls on the left. Everyone laughed and pushed and crowded to the tables, at last settling into place.

We quickly determined that at our table Tallahassee was the oldest and Becca the youngest. They brought the steaming platters of food to our table, then returned with large metal pitchers of apple juice and hot chocolate.

I helped myself to eggs and a couple of hotcakes. My mouth watered as the bacon tray slid past. I had never eaten pork in my life, not that we kept kosher, but simply by old tradition. My parents had never tasted it, either, I was sure. *Chazzar*, my mother called it, with a look of such profound disgust that it had never occurred to me to try it.

But I was away, up in the mountains in a new place, with new people and all sorts of new opportunities. Why not? You'll never know unless you try, I told myself, and I gingerly helped myself to a couple of slices of bacon.

Eggs, pancakes, everything was soon gone, but still the bacon lay there, curled at the edges, the white flesh looking too much like the poor pig that had sacrificed itself.

I glanced about; nobody cared about that limp offering, except for me. Guiltily I tore off a small piece; it felt greasy in my fingers. I popped it quickly into my mouth and swallowed, shuddered at the fat, then pushed the rest of it into my napkin and wadded the napkin into a ball.

"At home," said a voice behind me, "if we don't eat up, we get it the next meal."

I turned. It was Nancy Rae, looking down over my shoulder.

"Why'd you take that food if you didn't want to eat it?" Nancy Rae demanded.

I felt flustered, and I stammered, blushing, "I—I don't know."

"I know why," she said.

I braced myself for the attack. Jew! Jew! I had heard enough accusations, fought enough battles to recognize the look, the tone.

"You're a vegetarian, aren't you," she stated.

I let out a laugh, astonished and relieved and amazed at Nancy Rae's nerve.

"Well, yes," I said. The lie stung; I felt my face going red.

"My mom says vegetarians are crazy," said Nancy Rae. With that, she turned away.

Some people, I knew, believed in reincarnation. They said you meet the same souls over and over again, in different bodies, until you learn to get along. Was it possible that Nancy Rae and I had already hated each other in a different life? I almost laughed aloud and could hardly wait to share the thought with Tally.

Our counselor, Karen, came over to the table. "You kids," she said, "are going to be your own little group, and you get to sleep without a counselor, okay? They need me in with the ten- to twelve-year-olds next door. Just keep the place clean. There's inspection every morning at nine. Pick out a cabin name for yourselves and a cabin project."

"What sort of a project?" we asked.

"Mary will explain," said Karen with a smile. "Hey, you kids are so lucky," she said. "I was in a small cabin the year I was thirteen, just six of us. We're all still close. I guess we'll be friends forever."

I glanced around at Becca, Lenore, Tally, and Nancy Rae. I wished we'd gotten Sandra or Brittany or anybody but Nancy Rae—how could we ever become close with her around?

Nancy Rae was talking to several other girls from the next table. Maybe it was just me, I thought. For some reason, she seemed to dislike me from the first moment. Maybe I'd try to be nice to her. Try to understand her. But maybe she'd just think I was kissing up to her. I sighed.

"Announcements!" called out Douglas, the camp co-director. He talked about the various morning activities and introduced the counselors. Richard, a stocky, bearded young man, was in charge of the lake. Karen did crafts. Ed handled the horses. Sal, Douglas's wife, helped with all the housekeeping chores. Beatrice, the nurse, also led nature hikes and taught Indian lore.

"John Wright," announced Douglas, "is in charge of campfire programs. And Ellen Haymes—welcome back, Ellen!—is in charge of music this year, and I must say, we're delighted to have you, Ellen. Ellen! Come on up here and start us off with a song or two."

Ellen bounced up, her beautiful red hair bobbing. She strode to the front of the lodge, raised both arms for attention, and smiled that brilliant smile. She was dressed in tan walking shorts and a bright green sweater, over which she wore a pair of adorable red-and-green felt suspenders. I'd never seen anybody look so perfect, and when Ellen held up her hands for attention, it was obvious that everyone else thought she was perfect, too.

A couple of loud whistles pierced the air from the boys' side; Ellen merely smiled and tossed her head, a gesture of acknowledgment and modest acceptance and gratitude all combined.

"Hey, everybody!" Ellen called, smiling widely, "we'll warm up with a round. You all know 'Row, Row, Row Your Boat.' These three tables first, these three tables second . . ."

In a moment Ellen had everyone organized, and soon the dining hall rang with music.

John Wright kept the rhythm, clapping enthusiastically, and I saw Ellen give him a nod and a wink. Oh, she was fabulous. I would have given anything to be in her place. When Ellen went back to her table, three of her little campers embraced her as if she'd been gone for a week.

After the songs, Mary talked about cabin projects. "Look around," she said, "and see what needs to be done. We'll devote the first camp period each day to special projects. Almost everything you see here," Mary said, "except for the cabins themselves, was contributed by Quaker Pines campers through the years. The campfire circle, the lean-to at the lake, the wash stands, the playing field . . ."

"There's nothing left to do," called out a boy, and everyone laughed.

"Now, Tom," Mary answered the boy, "I'll bet you can think of a dozen projects. Last year," she told the rest of us, "Tom and his group made us a Ping-Pong table."

It was like a family. Mary was the mother. She knew everyone, it seemed, their abilities, their personalities. I wanted to belong, to do something special, to make Mary like me.

After breakfast the five of us wandered down to the campfire circle to plan our project and a cabin name. Not far from us the thirteen-year-old boys were meeting, too. We heard their laughter and their shouts; we knew they were watching and listening to us, too. And John Wright was with them.

"What would be a good cabin name?" Lenore asked.

"What kind of names do they usually choose?" I asked Tally.

"Oh, nature stuff," Tally said. "Like animals, usually. The little kids always choose Bunnies or Blue Jays or something like that."

"How about Bears?" suggested Becca.

Tally wrinkled her nose. "Not very feminine."

"Badgers?" suggested Lenore.

"No," I said. "That sounds like we badger people."

"How about Snakes," said Nancy Rae.

"No, no," we all said, "too negative."

"I don't know," I amended, glancing at Nancy Rae. "Maybe that isn't such a bad idea. We could think of a certain kind of snake, you know, like a cobra. Cobras are really interesting. They use them for snake charming and—"

"Oh, honestly," scoffed Nancy Rae. "I was only joking. Who'd want to have the name of a snake? A cobra, especially." She glanced all around, rolling her eyes.

Deep inside, I trembled with anger. I'd tried to be nice to Nancy Rae, and all I got was her scorn. Well, that's the last time, I thought.

"We could be Eagles," said Lenore, blinking behind her glasses. "They soar."

"Yeah!" exclaimed Tally. "It's perfect."

So we agreed. When it came to a project, I decided to speak right up. "We need a drain for those washbasins," I said. "It gets all muddy there, and the water just runs down the hill into a puddle."

"How do you make a drain?" asked Becca.

"We'd need pebbles," I began.

"You have to lay a pipe," interrupted Nancy Rae. "You dig a trench first."

We all stared at her; she really knew what she was talking about.

"Could we do it?" Lenore asked.

"Why not?" said Nancy Rae. "My dad does that stuff

all the time. I've watched him, gone with him a million times. You gotta get some rocks, too.''

We were all thrilled with our idea, and so was Mary when she came over to check. "Excellent," she said. "You can find pebbles galore over behind the lake. And back of the lodge there's a storeroom. You'll probably even find lengths of drainage pipe you can patch together. What a great idea, Nancy Rae!'' Mary laid her hand on Nancy Rae's shoulder.

"Thank you, Mary," said Nancy Rae sweetly.

I smoldered with resentment; it was my idea, after all.

The boys, who had named themselves Timber Wolves, were spying on us from behind the trees. They pranced, and teased, "Oh! Oh! I can see them digging a trench, can't you? Dear, dear, I got dirt on my hands—oh, my stars!''

Richard, their counselor, laughed and said, "Well, you guys better get busy with our own project, or the girls might just show you up.''

The boys kept goofing off. John Wright stood there listening and smiling at me. My cheeks burned, and I couldn't think of a thing to say. Finally he sauntered over and said, "I'm getting sign-ups for campfire shows. You girls want to sign up for a week from tonight? Next Saturday night?''

"We get to plan a whole show?'' I asked.

John smiled and I saw the tiniest dimple at the corner of his mouth, and his blue eyes sparkled. "Sure. You can write, direct, and perform it. I sort of thought you'd be interested.''

"What made you think so?'' I asked, allowing myself to actually look up at him. It had always been hard for me to look a handsome boy right in the eye.

"I heard you planning your project. You were taking charge.''

"What do you mean? I hardly said anything," I objected.

"You said enough. You just asked a couple of questions, got them thinking. It was your original idea, wasn't it?"

I tossed my head and smiled, trying to imitate Ellen's casual attitude.

"Tell me what you'll need for your show," said John. "I can help you get stuff together."

"How about a piano?" I asked, half teasing.

"Oh! You play!"

John's look was worth all those years of lessons and practicing.

"A little," I said, smiling modestly.

"Well, the last night of camp we usually have a musical. We can move Mary's piano out to the campfire circle. We could write some songs—want to?"

"Sure," I said, making my tone casual, though I was floating, soaring. Music and John Wright! What more could anybody want? Oh, Papa was right after all. He'd always said that if I knew how to play the piano I'd be the life of the party. People would gather around, singing while I played.

"Let me know when you get your show organized," John said. "Maybe I can help."

"Okay." I stood there awkwardly, suddenly struck dumb. Speak! I shouted to myself. Say something clever, cute, funny, intelligent! Nothing came.

Some people, I thought, always know what to say, how to say it. They draw people to them. They glow. John was like that. And Ellen. Superpeople, popular, always in control.

Whenever I saw Ellen or John, they were surrounded by admirers, both boys and girls. They knew everybody, always had a good word for everyone. It felt great to be in their orbit, just to get their smile.

Tally saw me, at lunch, unable to keep my eyes off John Wright. "Oh, boy," she whispered. "You've really got it bad—and it's only the second day!"

Mary had said we wouldn't have swimming until the following day because it takes time to get used to the altitude. Besides, Sunday was a day of quiet activities. After a brief service amid the pines, we read and walked and listened to records, and I learned my way around the camp.

The next day, at swim time, I got into my new bathing suit, a royal blue, one-piece latex with a sculpted top and a small bow in front. The suit made me look older, my legs long and well shaped. I realized now that since last spring I'd been growing pretty fast. Mama said that was what had given me the headaches. It wasn't my head that had grown, though. I turned to the side and admired my profile. Lisa had helped me shop for the bathing suit. In the dressing room she went into mock shock, clapping her hands to her face and using her Mammy routine to holler, "Ah do declahr, chile, yo getting a figure and that's fo' sure—you actshully sticks out in some places."

We laughed and then Lisa said, "Get it. It's perfect and you are gorgeous. Oh, Quaker Pines, look out—here comes Annie!"

I brushed my hair, which fell to my shoulders. People said my hair was my best feature. I took a deep breath, sucked in my stomach, and went outside.

As I stepped out into the sunlight, I pulled a large towel around my shoulders. I had never worn a bathing suit like this before, had never felt so exposed, so female.

Tally and several other girls came down the path, and I realized with a start that I was the only one wearing oxfords and socks. The rest had beach sandals. I felt mortified, but how could I hide my feet?

John Wright and a bunch of boys converged onto the path toward the lake. Half a dozen little boys were begging, "Teach me to dive, John. Will you play Marco Polo with us, John? Hey, John, race you across the lake!"

Those were the fateful words. "I'll race you across the lake, Annie," called Nancy Rae, running up behind me and Tally.

She walked briskly beside us. Her legs were long and skinny and pale, and she wore a knitted bathing suit, a sickening dark green. Inwardly, I gloated.

"Remember?" Nancy Rae said loudly. "You offered."

"Sure," I said, my mind shifting and jumping.

"You don't have to do it," Tally whispered. "That Nancy Rae is a pain in the you-know-what."

"I want to," I said.

Tallahassee eyed me suspiciously. "You know how to swim, don't you?"

"Yes," I said staunchly. "I do the sidestroke and the crawl."

"Good for you," said Tallahassee, and she yelled back to Nancy Rae, who by now had nearly caught up with John and the other boys, "Annie's gonna whip you, Nancy Rae! I'll bet you a dollar."

"You're on," yelled Nancy Rae. "Anyone else?"

"Forget it," said John. "Gambling's not allowed. But let's say we'll announce the winner at dinner tonight, and maybe get challengers, start a swim tournament."

"Great!" cried Nancy Rae. "You're on."

The lake, which looked silvery and cool from a distance, changed as we drew nearer. Water lapped continually in a brown fringe of mud at the edges. Patches of dark green algae looked slimy and horrid.

Several of the older boys and Richard, the counselor, were already swimming toward the raft that was anchored about midway. The raft bobbed roughly from side to side. I squinted out across the water, calculating; it must be four or five times the length of the Ambassador Hotel pool.

"Shall we race clear across?" I asked Nancy Rae, my voice steely, "Or do you want to race to the raft?"

"The raft," she said. I could see her nostrils swell with each breath, and her lips tightened grimly. "And back," she added. "We touch the raft with both hands, then turn. No stopping."

"We'll get wet first," I said. "Tally can say when." I put one foot into the water. It was absolutely freezing. The pebbles at the bottom pressed against the soles of my feet. I closed my eyes and plunged my body down into the water, feeling the shock of it. I screamed out, "Wow! It's freezing!" I opened my eyes to see the trees through the prisms of water dripping from my lashes, and then I heard Tallahassee calling loudly, "One for money, two for the show, three to get ready, four to *go!*"

I kicked off the bottom, shocked as the freezing water touched my face and head. I paddled swiftly, legs kicking, hands pulling, pulling, feeling as if I were caught in a whirlpool, for beside me the water was churned by Nancy Rae's swift, steady strokes. In moments her kicks sent waves of cold water lapping over my head, and when I looked up, I saw the foam made by her feet.

"Slow but sure," I told myself, recalling the story of the tortoise and the hare. "Save your strength, slow but sure, stroke, stroke, stroke, kick, kick, kick." I pulled at the water, lunged forward with each stroke, gulped in air, trying to establish a rhythm. I heard dull sounds behind me, and I realized it was the screams of the other campers, egging us on.

Go, go, go! The urgent cry beat itself into my lungs, my arms, my brain. *I can, I can, I can, I can*, echoed with every kick. One blink, and I saw that Nancy Rae was already far ahead of me. I plunged ahead, envisioning myself as a dolphin, a whale, a shark, wishing and willing it. Go! Go! But I seemed to be merely treading water, while Nancy Rae was more than halfway to the raft, moving as steadily as a fish in a stream.

Part of me has always believed it; you can do anything, anything, if you really set your mind to it. Try! Try! I coached myself, straining to delay defeat. I can do it! I told myself as I stroked and kicked. Slow but sure. Tortoise. Hare. I can do it. Do it. I can.

But then a band, or something, caught me around the chest and began to squeeze. I had visions of an octopus, and I nearly laughed, and my mouth and nose filled with huge gulps of water.

The squeezing weight upon my chest pressed harder, the weight of many bricks, of iron, a torture. It sucked out my breath. It pulled me down and down. Green and black muck oozed into my eyes. Noises rang in my ears. I was sucked down, weighted, into blackness.

Suddenly a strong hand gripped me. A powerful arm came around my middle. Someone held my chin up. "Relax, relax," he said. "Let me do the work. Relax. Breathe. Breathe, honey."

Next thing, I felt my body go flat against a hard surface—the raft. There was a leaping inside me, like tadpoles flipping from my ears down to my chest, up into my throat, and then I coughed and coughed, and someone pounded my back, and a man's voice asked, "Are you all right? Are you all right?"

I opened my eyes. It was Richard, crouched beside me on the raft, and another boy, one of the Timber Wolves. The boy looked scared, and I wondered why, and then I realized I had nearly drowned. Richard had saved me. I felt oddly as if I were looking down at my own body. I tried to speak and coughed violently.

Richard helped me sit up. He held my head while I coughed and coughed.

I nodded. "I'm okay." I pressed my lips tight together, so as not to cry. "I'm okay."

I gazed out to the shore, and saw that Nancy Rae was finishing the race, stepping out of the water, being wrapped in a large towel. A small rowboat came alongside the raft. In it was John Wright, and he thrust his hand toward me.

The two on the raft helped me into the boat, where I sank down, my teeth chattering.

John's face was set as he rowed, and I saw the muscles rippling at his cheeks and throat. "Are you okay?" he asked again and again. "Are you okay?"

By the time we got to the edge of the lake my entire body felt like ice, except for my hands and face, which were numb with cold, and I was shaking so hard that the small boat seemed to be shuddering along with my spasms. My new bathing suit was filthy with mud; pebbles and wet strings of algae clung to the front of it.

On shore, Douglas wrapped a sleeping bag around me and carried me, like a sack of potatoes, over his shoulder, past the shocked faces of the other campers, and I heard them begin to buzz and chatter.

I caught a glimpse of Ellen beside John. Her eyes were narrowed and she said, "What a stupid thing to do. Totally selfish. They ought to send her home."

6

Enemies and Friends

THEY TOOK ME TO MARY'S CABIN, THE ONE NEAREST THE lake. Mary immediately filled her bathtub with hot water, added suds, and pointed. "Get in. Quick. Or you'll catch your death of a chill."

Alice stood at the door, staring. "Out, Alice!" her mother commanded sharply. "The girl wants some privacy." To me Mary said, "I'll fix you a cup of hot tea. You just soak in there until you're good and ready to come out."

I sank down under the hot water, never before so grateful for warmth. My teeth still chattered. I felt like the world's biggest idiot. I would never forget that look on Ellen's face. My muddy bathing suit lay on the floor. My hair was sticky and smelly from the mud. I had looked like a drowned rat when John Wright came to rescue me. I wanted to hide forever.

I turned the hot water on to a trickle with my toe and watched the little trail of steam rising up, as life and feeling gradually crept back into my limbs.

I could have died, I suddenly realized, and a sick feeling came over me. How could I have been so foolish as to accept that challenge from Nancy Rae? I should have known I couldn't beat her—not at swimming. I realized now that Nancy Rae had to be an expert swimmer to do what she did. She might at least have warned me.

That she didn't care shocked me. I had trusted Nancy Rae to be decent and fair. Now, I only wanted revenge.

As if there were another person inside me, the arguments rang in my head: I shouldn't blame Nancy Rae. It was my own dumb fault for accepting the race. No, she tricked me. Her fault, my fault . . .

Voices filtered in from the other room, soft rumbles at first, then louder. I recognized Douglas, the codirector, and his wife, Sal, talking to Mary.

". . . a threat to other children . . . irresponsible . . . I mean, coming from such a background . . .

"Send her home . . ."

" . . . deprived . . . pathetic child . . . I say, nobody goes home. We work with them here. As we're pledged to do."

"Then you must take responsibility."

I heard no more, for I had let the water cover my head, warm and safe for an instant, away from shame. Deprived! Pathetic! Maybe we were poor, and we had our problems, but pathetic? I felt mortified. It was like the time that social worker came to the house and made us feel ashamed of being poor, needing to be lectured about how to spend our money, how to live. That was a long time ago, when we first arrived in America. But I never forgot how that social worker made us feel—like dirt.

As I emerged I heard the words, ". . . father is a brute, and I know they beat her."

Suddenly I realized it was Nancy Rae they were talking about, not me.

I shampooed my hair, then got out and washed the tub. Mary had left a thick brown terry-cloth robe for me, and a pair of fuzzy yellow slippers. I put them on, wound a towel around my hair, and went into the living room.

The others were gone. Mary sat on the sofa, drinking tea. "Sit down, Annie," she said. She pointed to the other cup of tea on the tray, and the iced cookies. "Help yourself."

I glanced at Mary, her long, slim legs, the soft blond hair pulled back from her narrow, sensitive face. She was not beautiful, but there was something captivating about her, strength combined with gentleness. It showed in the set of her chin, her large eyes, her mouth. I wondered how old she was—perhaps thirty-five, I thought, pretty old to have such a young child, old enough to be *my* mother, though she seemed more like an older sister.

I took the tea, sipped it slowly. "That's good," I said. I helped myself to a cookie. "Thank you so much."

"You're welcome." Mary smiled. "I love to bake," she said. "It's one of my vices."

"What's a vice?" I asked.

"Something you do to extremes, something you can't seem to help."

"Baking cookies doesn't seem like much of a vice," I said.

Mary laughed. "Not as bad as some, I'll admit."

I felt embarrassed. She meant being conceited, I sup-

posed, acting like a big shot when you should know better—
she'd start to lecture me now, about my vice.

Sighing, I glanced around the room. It was small, with a
stone fireplace and uneven floors covered with various small
rugs. The sofa and two chairs and coffee table took most of
the space, and along the wall were shelves filled with books
and piano music, to go with the upright piano. On the piano
were three photographs, one of Mary herself, beautiful and
smiling, her hair hanging loose, looking younger than she did
now. Two were of a man in uniform, Mary's husband, I was
sure. He had a thin mustache, the sort movie stars like Errol
Flynn wore, and he had beautiful, gentle eyes.

Alice came in, climbed onto the sofa beside me, asking
Mary, "I have a cookie, Mama?"

"Of course," said her mother. "I want to talk to Annie,"
she continued. "You run along and play in your room, then."

The child grabbed a basket full of crayons and a coloring
book and skipped away. "I'll draw Annie a picture," she
said over her shoulder, smiling at me.

I smiled back, then became serious when I saw Mary's
look, distant, troubled.

"Tell me, Annie," Mary said suddenly. "What do you
like to do best?"

The question startled me. I had expected Mary to scold
me for racing against Nancy Rae or anybody, when it was
obvious I couldn't swim worth a darn.

I frowned. Nobody had ever asked me that before. I began
slowly. "I like to be with my dog, Skippy. I wanted to work
for the vet, but he didn't need me. He said I should apply in
a couple of years, when I'm older. I love to play the piano,

but I'm not good enough to ever be professional. When I'm alone I write poems and stories.'' I blushed. It seemed silly.

Mary nodded. ''We have a lot in common, you and I,'' she said. Her tone was soft and easy, as if we were two grown women talking together and having tea, two friends. ''Have you been to the horses yet?''

''No.''

''Do you ride?''

''No. I've always wanted to. There's no horses near where I live.''

''Would you like to learn?'' Mary asked.

''Yes! I'd give anything!''

''Would you?'' Mary smiled. ''All right. I'll make a bargain with you. You may report to the stable every day right after rest time. Ed will teach you how to clean and groom the horses. That will be part of the bargain. You say you want to work with animals. It can be very filthy, hard work, mucking out the stalls, fetching water. Are you willing to try it?''

''Yes! Oh, yes.''

''Very well,'' Mary said. ''Every day, right after rest period, when the other campers choose their fourth period, you may go to the stable. My dogs are at the stable most of the time, too.''

''Dogs? Dogs?'' I could hardly believe it. ''How many?''

''Only two,'' Mary said with a smile. ''There are kittens up there, too. They're up in the loft with their mother, just born three days ago. I'll come down once in a while and give you some pointers about riding.''

I was ecstatic.

"Now comes the hard part," Mary said. "If you don't want to do it, or if you don't think you can, tell me honestly."

"All right." For Mary, I'd do anything, I thought, filled with love.

"I'd like you to include Nancy Rae in this project," Mary said, looking into my eyes very deeply, earnestly. "I want you to teach her about the animals. She's never had a pet."

"How do you know?" I asked.

"Just leave it to say that I—I know her family. I've been to her home. We sometimes make home visits to prospective campers."

My first reaction was to cry out, no, I wouldn't! Having Nancy Rae around would ruin everything. Why should I have to help Nancy Rae, when she nearly killed me? Nancy Rae hated me at first sight. She was probably laughing herself sick over my calamity.

"What do you say?" Mary asked gently.

I looked at Mary's serene face. "All right," I said.

"Good! You can start Friday, after camp gets into full swing." She got up briskly, picked up the telephone, and called the lodge to have somebody bring me dry clothing from my cabin.

"Tally's coming," Mary said. "It will take her a few minutes." Mary went to the piano. She opened the bench and brought out a book of music. "I have these duets," she said, "but nobody to play them with. Want to take a look?"

I glanced at the music. Simple, really, the sort of duets I'd played with Paula years ago.

"Let's try them," I said.

We sat down together on the bench, and Mary counted,

and before I knew it we were playing one song after another, I at the treble, Mary at the bass. Annie came running in to listen. We played some folk dances and a jig and a hunting song. When we were done, I heard clapping, and Tally stood there beaming.

"You're good, Annie!" Tallahassee exclaimed. "That was terrific."

"Those were easy songs," I shrugged.

Mary said softly, "Just say 'thank you,' Annie."

I looked up, startled. *Just say thank you*. Accept the compliment, she meant. Don't be down on yourself.

"Thank you," I said to Mary and Tallahassee both.

I changed my clothes, then gave Alice a quick hug good-bye, thinking she must be the luckiest little girl in the world.

As we walked back Tally said, "The whole camp's talking about you," she said. "You had a lot of guts."

"Thank you," I said with a grin. "One slight problem," I added. "I can't swim."

"I noticed."

We both laughed. It was good to be alive, to have a friend.

"I'm going to find Herbie," Tally said. "I promised him a game of tetherball. He needs the practice."

"Sure," I said. "Go ahead."

I walked on alone, grateful for these moments of silence. How beautiful the trees were! The sky was vast and very blue. At home, who had time to see the sky?

I thought of what Mary had said about Nancy Rae. I wanted, more than anything, to be like Mary, to make her proud of me. All right, I thought. I'll be nice to Nancy Rae if it kills me!

For the next couple of days I did my best to just forget about Nancy Rae. The only activity we did as a group was our project, and Nancy Rae was a hard worker. She carried buckets of pebbles over to our site; she took her turns along with the rest of us using the shovel and the pick. She seemed to like the hard work. Her face would get very red, and after the exertion, her freckles stood out sharply, and her round face was layered with sweat.

"My dad and me laid an entire driveway one morning; he taught me how to stir the cement," Nancy Rae boasted. "This here's easy as pie by comparison."

Whatever anybody did, Nancy Rae had done it better, longer, farther. And the truth was, she *was* strong. She would slide into base heedless of the gravel on the ground, and once, up at bat, she got hit in the head with the ball and came up gasping, mouth opened wide, actually laughing, and shouted, "Wait'll I tell my brother! He thinks he's so hot!"

She was a strong tetherball player, and she challenged everybody. She could shin all the way up the flagpole in eight seconds, then slide down, leaving long, red welts on her legs.

"Nancy Rae!" Becca exclaimed, looking at the burns, "doesn't that hurt?" Nancy Rae only tossed her head and laughed. "So what?"

It was almost as if Nancy Rae were trying to get hurt, to prove something. My parents always filled my ears with admonitions, cautioning me against getting hurt or breaking a bone, catching cold, having an accident. How many thousands of times I must have heard the words, "Be careful!" Apparently, nobody had ever said anything like that to Nancy Rae.

I'd watch her out of the corner of my eye, rolling her eyes

as she told some tale of daring—then I hated Nancy Rae for being a show-off, a daredevil. I was her opposite, held back by my parents, afraid to get hurt, a sissy, a coward.

But I was getting stronger each day. I got a base hit at the twilight baseball game, bringing in two runs. I went on the ten-mile hike that Richard led, and while some of the kids complained about blisters and aches, I felt terrific. If only Mama could see me now! On a before-breakfast walk, Beatrice taught a group of us how to recognize birds' calls and to track animals by their leavings. The world was opening before me. Quaker Pines was heaven, I thought, or it would have been if it wasn't for Nancy Rae. She spoiled everything with her whispers, her grudging looks, her grabbing, her bragging.

One day Tally had gone looking for Herbie again, and I was going to get my jacket for campfire. As I entered the cabin I heard voices coming from the alcove that Tally and I shared. I saw the shadows and shapes of four or five girls, some of them from another cabin.

I heard Nancy Rae's voice. "Look at the mess. My daddy says those niggers are worse than animals. And Annie's no better. She's dirty."

"Yeah, look at her junk," said another girl. "How can you stand to be in the same cabin?"

"Did you see her shoes? She goes swimming with her saddle oxfords on!" They laughed and laughed.

"And that jacket! She looks like Popeye in that jacket!"

I moved closer. Now I saw them all in a huddle, bent over my things. I saw Nancy Rae reach down under my pillow as if she knew exactly what she would find there: It was where I kept my private journal.

I shouted out, "What are you doing with my things?"

They all turned, then froze.

Nancy Rae gave a laugh. "Hey! Popeye! Wanna race me across the lake again?"

My pulse beat in my ears; I was ready to leap at her, to grab her hair, to kick and bite. But something slowed me down—the voice of reason telling me that I must not lose control of my temper, not this time. I held back.

But Nancy Rae must have seen it as weakness. Gathering her audience, she continued to taunt me. "You're a nigger lover, aren't you? Do you sleep in the same bed with your nigger friend? Jews and niggers . . ."

I lunged toward her, but suddenly, strong arms gripped me from behind. Tally was there, pulling me back.

"No!" she yelled. "Don't stoop to her level, Annie! She's just stupid. Forget it."

"I hate her!" I shouted, and rage overwhelmed me to the point that I could not even see where I was going.

We had left Germany to escape the persecution of the Nazis. And even here, there were bigoted and hateful people among us, people who would hurt and even kill just because someone seems different. I thought of the screaming, rock-throwing kids who used to chase me home from grammar school, taunting, "Dirty Jew! Sheeny, sheeny, killed my Lord!" I remembered my Japanese friend, Setsu, who was sent away with her family to some horrible camp in the desert—just because she was Japanese and some Americans classed them all as spies. They called them names, too, "Yellow Bellies" and "Japs," just as dark-skinned people were called names. And as Tally held me and spoke to me, soothing my hurt, I thought with shame of my own sister

Lisa, and the way she imitated Mammy, that long, stupid drawl, and how I had laughed and laughed with her, enjoying it. Now I was overcome with remorse added to my rage.

Tally pulled me outside and down along the path toward the campfire circle, now empty and silent.

I struggled against her, even as I knew I was out of control with anger. "Let me go! Let me go!" I pushed against her.

"Annie! Annie!" With great force, Tally held me back; I felt the strength of her muscles and she wrapped her arms around me. She was much taller than I, much larger, as was Nancy Rae.

"You could beat her up," I said, still panting. "She's such a coward. Picks on people who are smaller . . ."

"I wouldn't waste my time," said Tally. "Come on." We walked past our drainage project. It was going well. I remembered how we had sung a camp song while we worked:

> "How gladly together
> In all kinds of weather,
> My friend and my neighbor
> Together we labor
> To make the world brighter and fair."

"Nancy Rae spoils everything," I said.

Tally sat down on a log. I sat down beside her, poking at the decaying bark with a stick. "Hey," Tallahassee said, "if I fought every time somebody called me a name, I'd be black and blue—and with this skin, that's pretty hard to come by!" She laughed.

I stared at her, and I wished I didn't care, but anger still burned in me. "How does she know I'm Jewish?" I burst out. "Do I have a sign around my neck?"

"No. You're lucky. It doesn't show. She was probably just guessing."

I sighed deeply; things were obviously much worse for Tallahassee, yet she never let her temper get the best of her. I wanted to tell her about Lisa's imitation and my laughter. I wanted to confess, to be forgiven. But I said nothing, holding my guilty secret inside.

That night I pulled out my little journal and wrote down my feelings about Nancy Rae. I also wrote about Tally. It came out in a poem, quick and direct:

Friend

Some say we are not alike,
Opposite, like black and white,
But I have felt your touch and know
Our friendship will forever grow.

"What are you writing?" Tally asked softly.

"A poem," I whispered.

"Could you write me one?"

"I did," I said, embarrassed.

"Could I see it?"

"I guess so." I handed Tally the book.

She took it from me and read. When she turned her head to me again, I saw tears in her eyes. "That's beautiful," she whispered. "I knew, the minute you talked to me on the bus, we'd be friends."

"Me, too," I said. "There's another poem on the back page."

Tallahassee turned, found the back page, and read. " 'To J. W.' Uh-oh," she said. "You'll have real trouble if you-know-who gets hold of this."

"It's a love poem," I whispered.

"Looks like it," Tally said. I had drawn hearts and daisies all around the edge of the paper.

Holding her flashlight to the page, Tallahassee slowly read my poem. I watched her read, watched the look on her face, the slight widening of her eyes, her parted lips. She liked it; I could tell.

Tallahassee glanced at me, her brow puckered, then she read it again.

"This is beautiful," she whispered. I saw the white gleam of her eyes, the admiration in her smile, and I felt warm, full of sudden joy.

"Yes," Tallahassee whispered. "It should be a song, you know? On the radio. People would remember it. You'd be famous."

"Who wants to be famous?" I quipped. "Not me. You have to go around signing all those autographs, running to the bank every day with buckets full of money—huh! It's too darn much trouble."

We giggled and giggled, and I almost forgot about hating Nancy Rae.

7

The Daredevil Kid

ALL NIGHT I GALLOPED THROUGH MY DREAMS, TWISTING and leaping about in my sleeping bag. I remembered the stories I'd read, of girls taming wild horses, nursing sick horses back to health, helping colts being born, taking charge, riding "like the wind."

In the morning I awakened, tired and edgy; whatever it was those storybook girls had, it was obviously lacking in me. I was scared to death at the thought of mounting one of those huge horses, let alone riding at a gallop. I contemplated the horrible consequences of being thrown: brain concussion, broken legs, teeth knocked out, even paralysis. I hated my cowardice. I longed to be easy, relaxed, poised.

I considered begging off; I'd tell Mary I really wanted to learn to swim, to face my inadequacy. It would sound so noble after what had happened. No, I told myself, gritting my teeth. I tied my hair back, put on my jeans and hiking boots, and ran down to the stable, gloating, for Nancy Rae had fallen asleep on her bed during rest period, and it would take her some time to rise and get ready.

Mary's two dogs, Lady and Buckaroo, ran to the gate to meet me. I had romped with them on the road, and petted them as they lay in the lodge by the fire. Buckaroo was a mixed breed, about the size of a Labrador, but spotted black, white, and tan. Lady was an exquisite, dignified golden retriever, with beautiful "feathers" at her paws and throat.

The dogs came and sniffed me all over. I squatted down to feel their warm bodies close to mine, and let them lick my face.

Ed was at the stable, rubbing down a saddle with a large, darkened cloth. "Annie!" he called. "Come on, there's plenty to be done. Have you ever mucked out a stall? No? Well, let's start with the pleasantness, then go on to the duties, right? You've spent much time with horses?"

"None," I said, drawing back, for as he spoke Ed swung open one of the stalls and the odor of horse came rushing upon me. "This is Molly, Mary's favorite mare—a beauty, isn't she?"

The mare was a beautiful, glossy chestnut color, with a flowing brown mane and large, expressive eyes. She was a large horse, and she stood proudly, glancing over her shoulder, then she turned deliberately away, tail twitching.

"She doesn't seem to like me," I said, my voice quaking, for at that moment Molly gave a snort and a little kick with her hind foot.

"Molly!" Ed's hand came down, hard, on the horse's rump. "None of that, my lady. Now, you turn around and greet Annie properly. She's just trying to get the upper hand," he murmured.

To my astonishment, the horse turned daintily in the stall and showed herself, head down and docile. "There," said Ed, stroking the large forehead. "That's better. Annie, hand me that halter there."

I glanced at the peg on the wall beside us, guessing at what Ed meant. I took down a leather strap and handed it to him. Ed swung the halter over Molly's neck.

"Come on, my beauty," Ed sweet-talked the mare. "She's a little insulted today, aren't you, girl? Didn't get out to pasture this morning—I'm sorry, sweetheart. Come on, my pretty love," he crooned, holding out half an apple.

The horse nuzzled the apple, sucked it in, and began to eat with round, exaggerated chewing motions. I was enchanted. I had never been so close to a large animal, to the fascinating teeth, the puffs of breath, the heat of its body and those long, firm muscles.

"Ah, she knows I love her," Ed said, fondly patting Molly's nose.

I wanted to touch Molly's face. Later, I told myself. I felt enveloped by the odor and the warmth of the animal, enveloped and also overwhelmed with nervousness.

Ed handed me the reins. "Here," he said. "You lead her."

"M-me?" I stammered. "Lead—lead her? Now?" My mouth went dry with terror. I had imagined, somehow, taking part in such things later, much later.

Molly knew. Suddenly she tossed her head and pawed the ground. One blow from those enormous hooves could flatten me!

"Now, now," said Ed, "good girl. You hang on Annie. She's just testing you. You show 'er who's boss. Take her round over there and tie her to that post. Then we'll groom her. Soon you'll have her eatin' out of your hand. That's right. Be firm. She's big, but you're the smart one, remember that. You're the boss.''

Now or never, I thought, and I lifted my chin and began to walk. To my utter amazement, I heard the clomp, clomp of hooves behind me, and I felt the elation of having proved something, however slight. I tied the lead around the post. But Molly continued to move forward. I laid my hand against her flank and said in a firm, loud voice, ''Stop.''

It worked. Molly stopped. She stood staring at me with those enormous dark eyes as if to question my sudden power, then bobbed her head in good-natured acknowledgment. I wanted to leap and shout; instead, I turned to Ed and said, ''I'm ready.''

Ed brought out several brushes.

''Never worked with horses, is that it?'' he murmured. ''Well, you've got the touch, soon you'll be working her in the ring. Horses are just like people—takes a gentle touch, a lot of listening.''

''Listening?'' I echoed.

''Listen to the animal—it tells you what it needs, not only by sounds, but the way it moves, turns, watches you. Horses are not very intelligent creatures. They're easily frightened. A paper sack in the road, a bit of wood lying in the path, they can terrify a horse. You must constantly reassure it, talk to it, let it know you're there, taking charge. See?''

''I see.''

''Horses are like people. It's only when they're scared that they get mean. Give 'em love, and you'll see, they'll come to you like kittens.''

While he spoke, Ed took up two large brushes and began to groom Molly's back, going hand over hand in a half-circular motion. He showed me how to hold the mane and comb it, so that the hair wouldn't get tangled. I began, and as I worked I gradually felt wrapped in the rhythm and the pleasure of it—the smell of the horse and the hay, the intense heat of those flanks, the stiff hair, the horse's breath against my face, its quivering lips and nostrils. The horse seemed to pulsate with heat and life and energy. I was transported, brushing and combing and patting this horse, at last summoning the nerve to lay my head gently against its cheek, as I had imagined doing while reading all those many storybooks.

I looked up, feeling someone watching me.

It was John Wright. He smiled and came over, saying, "There's nothing like the real feel and smell of a horse."

I nodded. "I've just discovered that."

"Oh! From the way you worked with those brushes, I'd have thought you were an old hand at this."

"Well, it's exactly like my dog," I said, laughing, "all the same parts. Just a bit bigger. Smells a little different, too. Actually, it smells good."

"A lot of people don't think so," said John.

I felt a swift bond—we both liked the same things, the feel, the smell of the horse, the stable; I was in heaven.

"I like the smell of dogs, too," I said. "Especially puppies." Oh, how stupid, I reproached myself, alone with John Wright at last, unable to talk about anything but *smells*!

But John stepped closer to me, laughing, and said, "I know! They sort of smell like chickens, don't they?"

"Yes," I said. "And ducks. I had a duck once. It used to swim in the bathtub. Every time my sisters were getting ready to go out, they'd get so mad to find that duck swimming in the tub. Then they'd pull it out and it dripped all over. They never knew what to do with a wet duck.''

John laughed and laughed. ''That's a great story. What happened to the duck?''

''Oh, it packed up and left one day,'' I said. ''I think my sisters bought it a bus ticket to Timbuktu.'' I was amazed; suddenly I could talk to a boy!

''Sisters can be rough,'' John said. ''I should know. I've got two of them.''

''So do I!'' I exclaimed. ''Are you the youngest?''

John nodded. ''Yes. How about you?''

''Me, too!''

''There you go—we've got a lot in common. Do you want to go riding sometime?'' John smiled at me. I thought I'd absolutely faint.

I said, ''I don't really know how to ride. Mary was going to teach me.''

John said, ''Mary said to tell you she can't come today. So I'll take Molly out in the ring. Want to help me lunge her?''

''What's that?'' I asked, looking up at John, painfully aware of my ignorance.

''We tie a long rope to her halter, stand in the middle of the ring, and let Molly run in circles. It gives her good exercise. Want to try it?''

The thought of having that horse run circles around me while I held on to a rope was about as appealing as leaping down the Grand Canyon. But I heard the expectation in John's voice, and in that instant, another voice intruded.

''Hey, why didn't you wait for me?''

I was stunned back into reality, with murder in my heart; it was Nancy Rae. I had no idea how long she'd been standing there, but she looked somehow as if she'd been listening for ages.

"Hi, Nancy Rae," said John pleasantly. "Come on over here and get acquainted with Molly."

I saw Nancy Rae's face go dead white, saw her swallow hard. She was plain scared. Her freckles stood out darker than ever.

Lady, the golden retriever, ambled near, tail wagging expectantly.

In one swift gesture Nancy Rae pulled back her foot, gave a kick that landed on the dog's side.

"Lady!" I called, shocked. A lesser dog would have whimpered or barked; not Lady. Dignified, she walked out the barn door and around to the side, head high.

I looked at John, but he was putting the brushes away and saw none of this.

I was about to speak, when John came over. "Nancy Rae, want to take Molly out? First, though, we better check her feet. Did Ed show you how to do that, Annie?"

"No."

"I'll show you," said John. "Come on, Nancy Rae. You can try it, too."

Nancy Rae came toward us, her eyes flickering. She was scared. I could tell. She jumped back as the horse tossed its head at a fly, and then she tried to cover up.

"Look out, Annie," she angrily called. "You almost got me stepped on."

"Me?" I cried. "What'd I do?"

"Hey, you two, listen up," said John impartially. "Now,

this is how you clean their hooves—see this pick? Stand here, just behind the foreleg, and pick it up. So. Then you get down in there—press pretty hard, you can't hurt the horse. This part of the foot is very solid, almost like a horn.''

Nancy Rae wrinkled her nose. ''It stinks.''

John gave me a glance and a smile. ''Want to try, Annie?''

''Sure.'' I took the pick, and after a couple of attempts I managed to lift the horse's front foot and hold it between my legs as I'd seen John do. Molly shifted her weight. Silently I prayed, Don't lean on me, don't lean on me. I would fall over onto the stable floor, covered with muck; how Nancy Rae would laugh!

I braced myself, head down, and concentrated on that hoof, saw the dark groove, pressed down on the pick into the soft frog at the back, as John had shown me, all around the hoof, and I managed to get out a wad of greenish brown stuff. It dropped to the floor.

''Good job,'' said John. He touched my arm. I felt like dancing. Behind him, Nancy Rae looked stunned.

I led Molly out to the ring, feeling powerful and grand. Then the three of us stood in the middle of the ring, and John held the rope and let Molly run.

After a time he handed me the end of the rope, and to my amazement, the horse kept going around and around, light as air, but holding on made all the difference. I was part of this grand dance, feeling the vibration of hooves on the ground, the movements of the horse's body against the lead rope.

''Good, very good,'' John murmured. ''You're a natural, Annie.''

I watched the muscles of the horse, the way it leaned into

the turns, the flaring nostrils, and I wished it were only John and me alone in the center of the ring. I was aware of Nancy Rae standing there watching. I heard her breaths, quick and short.

John took the rope from me and said, "Let's give her a little rest."

The horse slowed to a trot, then a walk.

"I'm gonna ride her," said Nancy Rae suddenly.

"Bareback?" asked John, looking amused. "I don't think . . ."

Nancy Rae stepped back. She took a flying leap and, with two hands flat on Molly's back, hoisted herself up and over onto the horse. She grasped the mane tight with both hands, gave a hard kick to the horse's flanks, and took off.

I watched, dumbfounded. I knew Nancy Rae had never ridden a horse before in her life. I knew she was scared to death of horses. And yet, there she was, flying.

"That kid!" yelped John. "What a daredevil!"

I saw the admiration in his eyes as we watched Nancy Rae riding around and around the ring. Her hair had come loose from her braid and stood out behind her, and the faster she went the more she leaned onto the horse's back, and I heard her give a long, loud screech, "Yah-hooo!"

At last Nancy Rae and the horse came to a stop. Nancy Rae's face was red. Her shirt was stained with sweat, and her hair looked frizzy and wild.

John raised his hands to lift her down. "Boy," he said, "don't tell me you need lessons—you could give them!"

Nancy Rae held tight to John for a moment.

I thought I'd choke.

Later, Ed gave all of us shovels and showed Nancy Rae

and me how to muck out a stall. He was right; mucking is one of the dirtiest, nastiest jobs in the world.

I fell to it with a vengeance, working the anger out, lifting shovel after shovel full of horse leavings. And even while I had to admire what Nancy Rae had done, had to admit the girl had nerve, amazing nerve, I couldn't help the plan that nudged at my mind, first mild and lazy, then urgent and compelling.

It all unfolded—brilliant, wonderful, perfect revenge. I could already taste my victory.

8

Sweet Revenge

TALLY AND I DID MOST OF THE WORK ON OUR SKIT. LENORE was just too serious to create comedy, and Becca didn't enjoy writing. As for Nancy Rae, she was usually off playing tetherball or jumping on the trampoline. She'd be in the skit, she said, if she could have her own number.

It fell right into our plans. Tally and I had fits laughing about our cleverness. Lenore was doubtful. "I don't know—it's pretty awful." But she laughed.

"You've got to have a sense of humor to appreciate it," said Tallahassee. "We'll see about Nancy Rae. She claims to have everything else."

A week after the swimming incident, even Becca seemed to be getting tired of Nancy Rae and her bragging and bossiness. But Tallahassee and Lenore and I decided to keep our little secret from Becca, too. We wanted to be sure of making an impact, we told each other, laughing hysterically at the pun.

The skit was wonderful; everybody who saw us rehearsing

thought so. It was a spoof called "A Day at Quacker Mines."
The campers were coal miners, laboring at Quacker Mines,
and the foremen were ducks carrying whips and quacking out
orders. We got some of the Timber Wolves to be our actors.
We made beaks out of colored paper and collected feathers
for their hair.

What a fabulous time we had! I wrote almost the entire
script, with a little help from Tallahassee and approval from
John, who thought it was clever and ingenious.

We girls played the campers or miners. Each act made
fun of a different camp situation, like the mud and algae in
the lake, or the pancakes on cook's day off, which stuck to
our mouths like putty. We made fun of KP duty with a song
all in rhyme, which Lenore and I composed to the tune of
"Old MacDonald Had a Farm," and finally we spoofed the
icy water that ran from the spigots, even in the showers, with
a song written to the tune of "Home on the Range."

It was, John said, definitely the best song in the show,
featuring Nancy Rae. She rehearsed it in a dry, hillbilly voice,
and the rest of us joined in the chorus:

"Oh, give me a bath that is lovely and hot
Not a shower that's made out of ice.
I don't ask a lot, but a penguin I'm not,
Cold showers are not very nice.

Camp, camp in the hills,
Where you soon learn to live without frills.
I don't mind it plain,
But it gives me a pain
Whenever that cold water spills."

And then we ended in the customary vaudeville moan, *"All over me!"*

There were several more verses, to fit between three choruses of "Camp, camp in the hills." It was the last number in our skit, and we were certain it would create a sensation.

We tore newspapers into little strips and placed them in a bucket. One of the boys, Rudy, sat up in a tree over the stage. It was his job to empty the bucket of "water" over Nancy Rae for the finale. Nancy Rae rehearsed her song two or three times, then got bored and threatened to walk out of the show altogether. We sweet-talked her: Hers was the best part in the show, the finale, a solo. We praised her and pleaded with her. I felt like the world's biggest promoter. Nancy Rae complained about having to pick bits of newspaper out of her hair. Tally and I dared not look at each other. We were both grinning inside: Just wait.

I had worked on programs before, at school. There is nothing like doing a show—that delicious anticipation, the excitement of molding ideas into action, then seeing them all come together at the performance. I was in seventh heaven, especially with John at the sidelines, nodding and smiling approval.

John and I also started planning the program for the last night of camp. It was going to be a variety show. The wonderful thing was, John and I were so alike. We liked the same tunes, we laughed at the same jokes.

"We're a good team," John told me. "You've got some great ideas." It was true. We clicked, and I was exhilarated.

We sat under a tree in the meadow. My heart raced when his arm brushed aganst mine. Paradise, I thought, gazing at the way sunlight made the grass a very pale shade of green.

Little yellow wildflowers nodded on their stems, and far beyond, pine trees stood tall and dark and forever.

Above us, a squirrel clambered up a tree, screeching.

"We invaded its home," John said.

"Sorry, squirrel," I said.

John smiled.

"This is great," he said, leaning back against a tree trunk. "I love the mountains and the trees." He began to hum the song "Annie Laurie." I joined in with the words.

John said, "You know, the 'bonnie brae' in that song must be sort of like this meadow. Very green. I'd love to see Scotland someday."

"Me, too," I said. "I'd rather travel than anything. I want to go to China and Siam."

"China! Yes," he said, smiling. "That would be wonderful. I've made a promise to myself. I'm going to try to see every country in the world."

"That's impossible," I exclaimed.

Firmly he shook his head. "No. If you want to do something, you have to make a plan. You start by telling somebody. My telling you now makes it even more possible. I'm going to see every country in the world!"

"Then so will I!" I exclaimed, laughing.

"Promise?"

"Promise!" We stood up opposite each other, and John seemed about to reach out and give me a hug. But some of the youngest boys came running down into the meadow. They saw us and squealed, "John! Annie! Want to play capture the flag?"

John looked at me and shrugged. "Want to?"

"Why not?" I said, dusting myself off.

"Annie," the little kids called, "can we use your scarf for a flag?"

"Sure," I said, and one of the little eight-year-old boys came up and hugged me. I felt loving and motherly and strong.

I was so very happy, that for a few minutes I considered changing our skit. I knew Tally and Lenore would go along with whatever I suggested. It was, really, mostly my skit, with my songs and my ideas. I could change it, forget that grand finale, and I decided I would.

But later, as I was walking back to our cabin to get a jacket for the campfire, I heard a commotion from the tetherball mound. There was Herbie Davis, Tallahassee's little brother, straining, leaping at the ball, which flew high above him, while his opponent taunted him: "Hey, little bugger, jump higher, why don't you? What's wrong with you? Catch it! Catch it!"

It was Nancy Rae. She caught the ball, then socked it with all her might, making it spin around the pole. I knew exactly what Nancy Rae had in mind; she would give the ball one more terrific blow, catching poor Herbie in the head or even the face. I'd seen it done plenty of times on the playground at school. One kid even got two teeth knocked out.

I watched, momentarily frozen, unwilling to embarrass Herbie, but imagining how it would feel to get blasted in the face with that tetherball. The next instant I raced down the hill toward Nancy Rae, feeling the wind in my ears, then the blow against my chest as I intercepted the ball. My foot caught Nancy Rae around the ankle and sent her sprawling.

She came up from the dust, her fists swinging, and she screamed, "What'd you do that for! Nigger lover! Nigger lover!"

I clenched my fists. It would not be my first fight; I'd had one or two playground battles when I was younger. I was ready. But suddenly the supper bell clanged, and Douglas came rushing along the path. Seeing Douglas, Nancy Rae started to bawl and cry, "She knocked me down—what's the matter with her? Look at my knee! My knee!"

"Girls, girls," temporized Douglas, taking each of us by the arm. "Come to supper now. Let's all try to get along, there now, no harm done. No harm."

I went to wash up, shaken and furious. Just wait, I thought. Tomorrow's campfire would pay her back plenty.

The next evening Tallahassee and I left supper early to get everything ready. We assembled all our props and smudged our faces with charcoal, being miners. We wore orange cardboard visors printed with the words QUACKER MINES. We borrowed shovels and a pick from the camp tool-shed; we would carry those over our shoulders.

Tallahassee and I had one last secret mission to accomplish. We raced to it, panting, laughing, a little scared. Rudy, of course, knew. He was sworn to secrecy.

At last it was time.

Campers and counselors sat around the campfire. I peered out from the makeshift little curtain, and I watched the flickering of the flames and saw the happy faces of the campers, and I never wanted this moment to end. The moment just before the big moment is always the best one.

Douglas made a few announcements. Ellen led everyone

in a couple of songs. Then John got up and announced our skit.

"Let's hear it for the soaring Eagles!" he called. "These kids have been working on this skit all week," he said, "and I want to tell you, it's really terrific. Give 'em a hand . . . the Eagles, assisted by a few of the Timber Wolves—let's hear it! Yeah!"

Everyone cheered and stamped; some of the kids who had been to rehearsal told others, "This is great—just wait and see."

The first act involved the entire cast, ending with Becca and Lenore in the KP duet.

We all joined the number about the lake, making rowing motions as we sang.

Tallahassee had a solo for part of the pancake piece, and she was hilarious, hamming it up so much that even I, who had seen it a dozen times before, was doubled over laughing.

My words! My songs and direction! I was elated.

It was time for the last number. How quickly it all went! I stationed myself at the sidelines with the rest of the actors, giving the limelight to Nancy Rae, and ready to join in the chorus.

Nancy Rae wore a pair of tight black pants and a dark shirt; her face was nearly black with coal, all except for her eyes, which looked sultry with eye makeup. Her lips were painted a glowing red. She was a sight—her hair frizzed out, tall and slinky, all in black. Nancy Rae brought to the song an accent I had never heard before, a mixture of hillbilly and southern, whine and wail.

Nancy Rae hadn't a drop of stage fright in her. She belted

out that song, using her hands and arms and hips, and the kids loved it. They hooted and howled, laughed and clapped, and the boys whistled. Above the stage sat Rudy, the bucket balanced beside him on the limb, and he glanced at me, waiting for the nod that I would give as the last chorus neared its end. . . .

". . . I don't mind it plain,
But it gives me a pain,
Whenever that cold water spills . . .
All over me!"

I gave the cue.

Rudy emptied the bucket.

Stable muck slid all over Nancy Rae, head, shoulders, chest, and feet.

For a long moment, time seemed to be sliced in half—empty space and silence hung over everyone. Then came Nancy Rae's howl. "Aowww! Sheeit!"

The campers went positively wild.

I don't know exactly what happened to Nancy Rae that night. The rest of us spent a long time laughing and celebrating, reliving our success. People kept on congratulating us. John Wright said ours was the funniest skit that had ever been performed at Quaker Pines.

Of course, we figured Nancy Rae was mad. We figured she asked Karen if she could sleep in the other cabin. We told each other what a bad sport she was, that she deserved it, that she should have been able to take a joke.

The next day being Sunday, we all met at Chapel Glen before breakfast for a brief religious service. We all wore white shirts, as we'd been instructed. Somebody played an old pump organ. I heard it, together with the strains of a flute, as quietly we walked across the camp grounds and down a gentle hill to the leafy glade, where logs had been laid in a semicircle and people sat quietly, listening.

The Quaker service is simple and direct. Nobody leads; there are no ministers or priests. There is music, an aid to meditation. People may rise and speak, sharing their thoughts, their hopes. Otherwise, it is a quiet reflection, serene and highly personal.

Tally and I sat in the chapel circle listening to the music, and I couldn't help thinking of the night past, my success, my gladness. Thank you! I sang inward praises. I felt that I had been vindicated.

After a time I heard the crunch of tires on gravel, the swift beep of a horn. Heads turned; people murmured.

Douglas, seated at the organ, turned to give Sal a nod. Sal slipped away from the group. I heard footsteps receding as she went up the hill.

I looked about. "Where's Nancy Rae?" I whispered to Tallahassee.

Tallahassee shrugged. "Karen's not here, either," she whispered.

"Shh!" several voices chided us, and we became silent at once.

I turned and saw Mary standing at the edge of the clearing. She wore white pants and a white shirt, the sleeves partly rolled, and a pale blue scarf around her hair. She looked very beautiful among the trees, almost unreal. Then her eyes met mine. I felt a jolt of uneasiness. Mary stood motionless, her body rigid, her mouth firm.

Richard rose and spoke briefly. "We are grateful for these times together in God's beauty. We are thankful for the woods, the sky, and the earth. Especially we are grateful for one another. Let us all come to know one another, reaching beyond the outer shell to the real person, the inner person. It is possible to love everyone when we reach deep into the soul."

No, I thought. It can't be possible to love everyone. Some people are mean and evil; how can we love them? Why should we?

I thought of Nancy Rae, and I wondered how long it would take for her to show her face again, and I even imagined that we'd end up laughing about the incident together. After all, she hadn't really been hurt.

Suddenly Mary's gentle voice rang out over the glade.

"I have read, in the Old Testament, something very wise," said Mary. "It says, 'Do not rejoice when your enemy falls. For your enemy is also the child of God, and beloved by Him.' How beautiful the world will be," Mary continued, "when we are no longer divided into enemies and friends. Let us begin here, today, to eliminate those divisions."

We sat in silence once more.

One or two of the junior counselors spoke about their gratitude for being here at Quaker Pines. Then the organ and flute played another hymn; Douglas motioned for everyone to rise, and people stood up and began to move out of the glen.

"Annie."

It was Mary's voice. I turned.

"Wait with me," Mary said.

I went to her, and we stood watching the other campers file past, until we two were the only ones left in the little glade, and then Mary sat down on a log and motioned for me to join her.

"Nancy Rae left camp this morning," Mary said.

I felt a jolt of surprise and let out a gasp.

"She called her father last night and asked him to come and get her. She was very upset, as you can imagine. She went into the cabin and packed her things while the rest of us were at chapel. You might have heard the car."

"I—I—," I stammered, and the sunlight flashed painfully into my eyes. I wished Mary would stop talking. I needed time to think, to confront this news. But no matter how much time we took, I now realized that something was broken beyond mending.

"I can't blame her," Mary continued. "To be humiliated in front of the entire camp—"

"She humiliated me!" I burst out. "Nancy Rae talked behind my back. She knew I couldn't swim, and she nearly got me drowned. She picked on me from the first moment, called me horrible names, lined up people against me."

"She made you her enemy," Mary said.

"Yes! Yes! She did!" I cried. "I even tried to be nice to her. She wouldn't—"

"And now you have lost the chance," said Mary, "to win her over as a friend."

"I don't care! I don't want her friendship."

"You will care, Annie. I know you will. Because you're not a mean person."

"Mary, Nancy Rae was mean to everyone."

"I know it. Annie, it was the only way she knew to get attention. You're the lucky one. You have talent."

"So does she! She's a great swimmer!"

"But she didn't understand how to use her abilities, Annie. I hope you do."

I was stunned, speechless as Mary began to move away from me, and I watched the whiteness of her clothes blending into the trees.

"Mary! Mary!" I called.

I sank down, crying and crying, and for the first time in my life I felt that I had no place in the world to hide. Exposed were all my ugly faults; there seemed no way ever to atone.

After a time I felt Mary's arm around me, a quick moment of warmth. Mary's touch plunged me deeper into despair than any punishment could have done. I cried and cried, feeling such shame and regret and dread of what might happen to me now.

"Come to breakfast," Mary said, pulling away.

"How can I?" I gasped. Everyone would stare at me, knowing I'd been crying.

"You must," she said firmly.

I rushed to the washbasins, splashed my face quickly with the icy cold water. Of course, it made me think of our skit, the song, and Nancy Rae.

I went into the lodge. I slipped into my place at the table, between Lenore and Tallahassee.

"What happened?" they asked. "Is Mary mad? What'd she say?"

"Nothing," I murmured.

Tallahassee said, "One of the boys heard Nancy Rae

talking on the phone last night. Campers aren't allowed to use the phones; Nancy Rae did it anyhow.''

"She told her dad," said Lenore, "that he better come get her.''

"She told him," added Tallahassee with a grin, " 'Daddy, there ain't nothing here but niggers and Baptists and Jews—you better come get me right away!' ''

I stared at Tallahassee. Could that be true? She was laughing. It was all a silly joke to her.

"Well, that's that," said Becca. "Good riddance. She was a real pain.''

I said nothing. Nothing at all. I kept seeing Nancy Rae in my mind, that broad, freckled face of hers, the way her hair was pulled so tight from her forehead. I saw again the hatred in her pale eyes, the swell of her small nostrils, and I remembered how she had belted out that song, expecting applause and receiving instead—the worst dose of embarrassment that anyone could imagine.

That night the empty bed and bare mattress confronted me and reproached me. I had been cruel.

9

Riding like the Wind

AFTER THAT INCIDENT WITH NANCY RAE, NOBODY MEN-
tioned it again. Mary received me in her cabin as before;
Sal and Douglas didn't hold any grudge against me. I was
amazed—and filled with gratitude and new energy.

We finished our camp project, the drain. The day we
finished, Mary announced it at dinner, and we Eagles soared
with pride. Then I had a new idea, more in line with my
talents.

"Let's start a camp newspaper," I suggested to my cabin
group.

"Oh, that's fine for you," said Tallahassee. "You love
to write. What about the rest of us?"

"You can distribute the paper," I replied. "Or duplicate
it. You can gather news."

Mary was dubious at first, with only two weeks of camp
left. Then she smiled and said, "Why not? You can start the
paper now, anyway, and leave a good beginning for next
year."

Next year! All at once my life had continuity. I imagined summer after summer at Quaker Pines, growing to be like the counselors I so admired, learning nature lore, tending the horses. Suddenly my life had a meaning all its own.

With Mary's approval, the idea of the newspaper took off. The other girls crowded around me with plans and encouragement. The masthead of the newspaper would read: *Founded by the Eagles, Summer 1945.* The newspaper might continue for decades, forever! We loved the idea of forever.

Everyone thought a camp newspaper was a wonderful idea, especially John Wright. "I've always thought we should have a camp paper," he said, "but nobody ever had the ambition to start one. What would we call it?"

"The *Quaker Quacker*," I said immediately, watching for John's reaction.

He burst out laughing. "Perfect! We can get somebody to draw a logo—maybe a duck reading the news. What's going to be in it?"

"We can print contest awards, game scores, news about the cabin projects. We'll have different columns, like 'The World at Large.' Richard's always listening to his radio. He could give us some news. We'll have jokes and riddles and poems—you'll see. Once you start a newspaper, you always find more news than you have space to print."

"You sound experienced," said John with a smile.

"I used to have a neighborhood newspaper," I confessed, "when I was only ten."

"What happened to it?" John asked.

"Well, I sold it for three cents a copy. But I wasted so much paper that it cost me about seven cents to produce. A business like that doesn't last long."

"How old are you, Annie?" John suddenly asked.

"Thirteen." I was embarrassed to meet his eyes.

"You've done lots of things, haven't you?"

We were in the lodge, outside the office. John put his hand on my back. I felt the warmth of his touch rushing through me. How desperately I wanted to move even closer to him! But my cheeks burned. I stepped back, looking away from John to the trees outside. How could it be possible to touch a boy, to feel all these feelings rushing about inside, and still look at his face?

Sal came out from the office and said, "You'll use the supply closet, there. It's full of paper and hectograph stencils, staples, everything you need. Do you know how to use the machine?"

"Yes," I said. For years I'd been helping teachers after school with chores like these.

"Then I now appoint you," said Sal grandly, "editor in chief of the *Quaker Quacker*. Congratulations, Annie. Douglas will announce it tonight at suppertime. You and your staff can meet every evening before campfire. You'll have to give up a camp period to do the editing and layout."

I laughed. "Something tells me I should give up swimming."

"I think everyone here would agree," said Sal with a grin, and she disappeared into the storeroom again.

"Now you'll have to pick yourself a staff of reporters," said John lightly. "I'd be happy to volunteer as one of your slaves."

My heart was thumping. "Sure," I said, making my voice very breezy. "You can be in charge of the jokes—or would you rather do advice to the lovelorn?"

"Jokes would be better for me," he said. "I don't know much about love."

"Someone should teach you," I said, amazed at my boldness.

"Are you volunteering?"

I was spared an answer when Sal once again emerged to point out the materials.

I began to dream about John, to think about when I'd see him again, and where, imagining what he'd say, what I'd reply, imaging how it might feel if he were to kiss me under the trees, to touch me, hold me, and talk about love.

I signed up for the hikes he was leading, even if it meant I had to bring up the rear with a bunch of little kids. It was worth it to be near John. I kept making suggestions for the last campfire program, insisting on more rehearsals, so we could be together. After lights-out Tallahassee and I lay in bed talking about John, then I dreamed his love all night.

One afternoon, the fourth week of camp, I went to the stable after rest time, hoping to find John there. We'd never yet had time for that ride together. Mary and John and Ed had all worked with me, teaching me to ride in the ring, and once or twice Ed had taken me out with just two other campers. But to ride free, to ride with John in the meadow—that seemed idyllic, like a storybook scene.

I looked down at my hands, callused and darkened now from work. For the past weeks I had spent some time every day at the barns, grooming, pitching hay, mucking out stalls, riding, climbing up into the loft to play with the kittens, bringing them down for Alice to hold. Ellen would bring in her eight-year-old campers. They begged me to show them the kittens or to help them feed a bit of bread or carrot to the horses. Of all the talent Ellen possessed, she had no feel for animals. She cringed when the dogs ran up to her, and when I saddled a horse she watched, looking bewildered and almost awed.

Sometimes I helped the younger campers in the ring, holding the horse's rope, with Ed or Mary watching, of course. Then, I felt alive and strong, and any thoughts of home were far, far distant. Was it possible that the house still stood exactly as before? That they all were going on about their lives, almost unchanging, while I was becoming a new person?

Letters from home were short and ordinary. "Dear Annie," Mama wrote, "How are you? We are all fine. Skippy is fine. We have the baby here and she is very sweet. Be careful when you swim or hike. Do not go alone into the forest. I love you very much. Your Mother."

I wrote back postcards, too busy for letters. During rest time I preferred to write in my journal. If I told Mama about my work at the stable, she'd only be worried, and Papa would say I was too wild. So I wrote brief, sparse notes home and saved my adventures for the journal. I thought of Lisa and her beautifully manicured fingernails, and how she would scold to see me now, looking more like a tomboy than ever.

I was amazed at how much I'd learned in the past weeks. I could saddle up and bridle the horses now all alone, even tightening the girth exactly right. Ed checked the hooves and coats of the horses I groomed. His highest praise came in the form of a grin and an okay sign. "You've got the touch, Annie," he said.

Mary praised me, too, for cleaning up the tack room and

saddle-soaping the harnesses. "Everything looks so fresh," Mary said. "The place obviously needed your touch."

I warmed at her compliment. Since Nancy Rae's departure, I felt especially tender, waiting for some final judgment.

Now I walked down the hillside, entered the big barn. Nobody seemed to be around. I remembered then, it was Wednesday, the day Ed always went to town for supplies. He was obviously held up. Campers weren't allowed alone at the stables, but I expected John at any moment, and maybe Mary, too.

I went to Molly's stall with a roll I'd brought from lunch. I stroked Molly's tough hide, her mane, the place between her eyes. Molly nuzzled my shoulder, looking for food and affection. I gave her the roll and watched her large teeth grinding on it, saw the fog of her breath, the greenish gloss of her lip, smelled the dense odor of her, and felt supremely happy.

I glanced at the large clock: five after two. In a minute or so John would be here, perhaps with a group of campers. I decided to get one of the saddles I'd been working on yesterday, but had left unfinished.

I brought the saddle over to the post, and from the shelf I took the cloth and the saddle soap and set to work.

Suddenly I heard a noise. The tack room door swung open. I was startled; one of the dogs, I thought, expecting Buck or Lady to come leaping at me.

But when I turned, there in the shadows stood Slim, one of the kitchen helpers. He was at least twenty, always smiling, but in an eerie way; I had never heard him speak before. Now he stood looking at me with open curiosity. "Hi," he said.

His dark hair was combed straight down over his forehead. He wore a white shirt, the sleeves rolled up, and jeans.
He was smiling. He leaned strangely to one side, his hand on
his hip, and his head was cocked, too, as if he were apprais-
ing me.

"Hi," I said, and I turned back to my polishing.

"Thought I'd bring some scraps to the animals," Slim
said.

That seemed strange; none of the kitchen staff did that
before.

"What did you bring?" I asked, for Slim kept staring
at me.

"Bones," he said. He held a bag in one hand.

"Horses don't eat meat," I told him. "Just vegetables.
You could give the bones to the dogs," I said.

"The dogs ain't here," Slim said, scratching his side.

I had wondered where the dogs were, but then, it wasn't
unusual for them to be roaming the hills looking for rabbits
and squirrels to chase. Now, I wished desperately for their
presence. Even Molly shifted nervously in her stall; I heard
the scraping of her hooves from behind me.

I picked up the saddle to replace it on its post, and in that
moment Slim moved toward me with a strange, swaying gait.
Something in me gave warning; but he leaped. So stunned
was I that I froze, mind and body both, while his hands came
up my sides and across to my breasts, and I felt his breath
against my neck while he whispered words and phrases I
hardly understood, so tangled and terrified were my thoughts.

Run. That single thought came pulsing through me. Run.

But Slim's grip tightened around my waist, and the heat
of his body seemed to overwhelm me, and his closeness, the

very smell of him, acid and unclean, seemed to blot out everything.

I went limp. He must have thought it meant acquiescence. His breathing quickened, and his words were harsh whispers, urgent and crude. I turned my face slightly; his mouth came down over mine, hot and wet, and in that instant I surged forward and flung the saddle down, hard, against his shins.

Slim fell backward, his face twisted in pain and astonishment. He yelled, cursed, staggered, then lunged toward me, ready for revenge.

But I had already reached the stall, swung open the door, and using the gate for a foothold, hoisted myself up onto Molly's back. "Go!" I shouted, giving a kick, and I laid my head down across Molly's neck and grasped her mane the way Nancy Rae had done.

Out the barn door she ran, with Slim staggering after us, but Molly was swiftly trotting, then moving into a canter as we cleared the barn door, headed up the road around the side of the stables to the meadow.

It was the most terrifying, exhilarating, awful, and wonderful ride I would ever experience. At first I felt nothing, saw nothing but streaks of green zipping past my line of vision. I still trembled with anger and fear, and I felt the muscles of my legs twitching against Molly's sides. My heart lunged with each motion of the horse; my breath was knocked out of my chest. I'll fall, I thought, fall . . . but with a curious sense of awe and almost detachment. If I fall . . . she'll trample me . . . I'll die . . . if I fall. . . .

And somehow it happened that everything slowed down; the trees still streaked past, but something in me became silent and composed, and the world went by with me at the center. Suddenly I knew that nothing bad would happen to me. I was strong. I could help myself. I could ride like the wind, and more.

When at last Molly slowed of her own volition, I relaxed my grip a little and sat up tall. Molly slowed to a walk. My breathing returned to normal. Amazed, I looked around, realizing that the world still stood, safe and sturdy, and I was okay.

I straightened up even higher, flexed my knees, controlling the horse, bringing her up the path toward the barn.

At the gate, his foot up on a bale of hay, stood John Wright.

Molly and I came over. I stared at John, then smiled.

"Guess you don't need riding lessons from me," he said.

"Guess not," I said.

I slipped down from Molly. She was frothing. I felt exhausted, suddenly. "Take her for me?"

"Sure," John said. "I'll have to walk her around and cool her off."

I got a halter out of the barn, slipped it around Molly's neck, gave the end to John. With a large towel I rubbed Molly's flanks.

John watched me closely. "Are you okay?" he asked.

"I'm fine."

John shrugged, rubbed the back of his neck. "I thought I saw some guy running away toward the bunkhouses."

I said nothing.

"Want to go riding tomorrow?" John asked. "With full saddle and bridle, that is?" He smiled.

"Sure," I said. My knees felt weak; all I wanted was to get back to my cabin and then take a shower. My legs were beginning to ache, and I was starting to discover how painful bareback riding can be.

"Annie!" John said. "Want me to walk you back?"

I turned, looked into his eyes. Now I felt truly shaken. I wondered what John knew, what he'd seen.

"No thanks," I whispered. "I'm okay."

"Very, very okay," John said. He leaned toward me, swiftly touched his lips to mine.

It was totally unexpected. Dazzling. I turned and ran.

It *was* a kiss, I told myself—no, not a *real* kiss. Yes it was. No it wasn't; it was too short. It was not romantic. The kind of kiss you give a child or a puppy, or a friend. It was a kiss, though, a definite kiss. No. Yes. No.

I shuffled through the arguments as I walked back, elated, confused, embarrassed, and when I got into the shower I let the cold water run on and on, until my whole body tingled.

Finally I got out, and as I stood on the cold, cracked cement of the shower room floor, I suddenly began to shake. I realized how close I had come to being in real trouble, alone in that barn with Slim. And on the heels of that horrible, unwanted touching, had come the touch I'd yearned for, John's tender kiss.

Still shivering, I put on clean clothes and ran to find Tally. She was in the crafts shop, making an ashtray out of clay for her dad. It was in the shape of a large leaf, and very artistic.

I complimented her, but I must still have looked pale, for she hastily put away her handiwork and drew me outside. "What's wrong?" she asked, fists clenched, as if she would fight off my enemies. "You look like you've seen a ghost."

"I—he kissed me," I whispered.

Tally's eyes widened and she gave me a grin. In accord,

we ran lightly down the slope, through the lacy trees to Chapel Glen, where we sat on a log, face to face, and I told her everything.

Slim's sudden, awful nearness, then John's lips touching mine. "How can a person feel so different about . . . I mean, I couldn't stand being near Slim, smelling his breath. Everything about him was so disgusting, Tally! But when John kissed me, it was, it was . . ." I could only sigh.

Tally nodded. "I know. It all depends on who does it, and how. It could be awful or—wonderful. Being close."

"I never expected anyone to—to just grab me like that. Oh, my mom's always warning me to be careful but—has that ever happened to you?" I asked.

Tally shook her head, but she didn't answer. "Boys are like that," she said grimly. "They always want to—you know."

"He's a man," I replied angrily. "He's at least twenty. He should have known better."

"He thought you were an easy mark," Tally said. "You have to watch yourself."

"I realize," I nodded. "It was stupid of me to be in the barn alone. But," I added bitterly, "why should I have to be afraid to go places? It isn't right! Why should I be the one to give up doing what I want, just because there are jerks like Slim around?"

Again Tally shook her head, and she looked much older now, and wise. "Can't explain it," she said. "It isn't fair. That's how it is—until we change it."

"Change it? How?"

Tally paused, frowning. "I don't know yet. I know my daddy always taught us to take care of ourselves. There's places you better not go and things you better not do, and it's just plain stupid to take stupid chances, he says.'' She smiled. ''My daddy got himself too many wives, that's for sure, but he always stayed on to take care of us.''

''What do you mean,'' I asked, ''about changing it?''

''Well, if guys like Slim keep getting away with that stuff . . .''

''Not this time,'' I said.

''What are you going to do about it?'' she asked. ''Listen, I didn't mean for you to get yourself in trouble. You probably gave him enough to think about, with that saddle landing on his whatever it landed on.'' She laughed wickedly.

''He shouldn't have been there,'' I argued. ''He should not have touched me.''

''Guys are like that,'' Tally said.

''They shouldn't be. I'm telling Mary,'' I said.

''You weren't supposed to be in the barn alone,'' Tally pointed out. ''You might get in trouble.''

''I know.''

It was late afternoon when finally I knocked at Mary's door.

''Annie! Good to see you; you must have read my mind. I was thinking about you. Alice is in bed with a cold, and she's longing for company.''

''I'll go in to her,'' I said. Then I added, ''But I have to tell you something first.'' After Mary heard, she might not want me there; I had disobeyed a camp rule, being at the stable alone. What happened as a result was partly my own fault.

It was difficult to say the words. I felt my cheeks stinging. I did not look at Mary as I concluded, ''He . . . grabbed me and touched me and said—awful things, so I threw the saddle at him and got onto Molly and rode out."

I could feel Mary staring at me, weighing what I had told her. "You used Molly to—to escape?"

"Yes."

"Bareback?"

"Yes."

"No bridle?"

I nodded.

"Good heavens, girl, where in the world does anybody learn to do that? You must have been terrified! But still . . ."

"Nancy Rae did it," I said. "To impress John."

"Well, I'll bet she succeeded!" Mary exclaimed.

"She impressed me, too," I said. "I'll never forget it."

I looked up at Mary. She was smiling, beaming, actually. "I never fail to be amazed at my campers," she said. "Well, go on in and see our little girl, won't you? There's a dish of rice pudding on the bureau. She's refused to eat anything all day. Maybe she'll take it from you."

I played fish with Alice, then put on her hand puppet and fed her rice pudding. She loved my performance, and ate every bite. I left her then, for I heard the campers giving their final cheers for their baseball teams. It was nearly suppertime.

Mary sat in the shadows, knitting a square for an afghan. I had never seen anybody knit so quickly, yet every stitch was perfect.

"That's beautiful," I said.

She sighed. "Keeps my hands busy, at least," she said.

"Is this the first one you've made?"

"Oh, dear me, no. It's the sixth."

I sensed a sudden heaviness here, and I was full of questions, but was half afraid to ask.

I glanced around the room. My eyes fastened on the photograph, as if Mary had somehow led me to it with her thoughts. I knew something was wrong.

"Alice's father?" I whispered.

Mary nodded. "He never saw Alice," Mary said. "He was shot down behind enemy lines. At the beginning of the war. He was a medic."

"A doctor?"

"No—a field medic, because Quakers don't fight, won't kill."

"Not even when they are at war?" I asked. "When they are attacked?"

Mary shook her head. "I couldn't understand it, either. He said he had to go to help—but he wouldn't carry a gun. Now," Mary said, "I think I understand. So I decided, in a small way at least, to continue his work here, at camp with the Quakers. He was a peaceable man," she said quietly.

I sighed deeply. "And the blankets?"

"I made the blankets for our boys fighting in Europe. I was planning to send this one over to the Pacific. But if my prayers are answered," she said with a trace of a smile, "maybe I won't have to send this one. What a time that will be, when our men come home, and we won't make war anymore!"

I nodded. We talked. I told her about my grandmother, how she had died. I told her about my cousins, aunts, and uncles. "They were all taken away," I said. "To concentration camps. My grandma was seventy-five years old when they took her away. We think they are all dead."

"War," she said. Only that single word. Neither of us needed to say more. It seemed grotesque that war could reach even to these mountains.

After campfire that night Mary made an announcement. "There is a slight personnel change in the kitchen," she said. "Slim is no longer with us. In his place we have a young man coming from Riverside tomorrow. Meanwhile, I want to remind all you younger campers, that if you want some pointers on grooming and riding and horses in general, talk to Annie Platt; she's at the stable every day after rest period. Also, *Quaker Quacker* staff, don't forget, you want to get your stories in to Annie by Thursday for Friday printing and distribution." Mary caught my eye and added, "How did we ever get along without Annie?"

Ellen got up to lead the camp in a final song. She looked beautiful in the firelight, filled with energy, as usual, commanding all eyes and all voices.

But for the first time, I looked at Ellen with something more than envy. She's terrific, I thought. And I gathered my breath to sing out with the others, loud and strong.

But there is always a thorn among the roses, as the storybooks say: Back from campfire, I trudged out of our cabin with flashlight in hand, to get some water in my canteen. It was there that I saw Ellen in the moonlight, holding hands, walking very slowly and close together with John Wright.

That night Tally and I talked and talked. She listened for hours to my whispered grief. "That's how it is," she said over and over. "John's just so sweet to everybody. Makes you think you're the only one. He likes you, Annie. Just because he likes Ellen, too . . . he did kiss you."

"Why did he kiss me?" I moaned.

"He just wanted to," Tally said. "Didn't you like it?"

"Yes. Of course. It made me feel all . . ."

"Squishy inside?" Tally suggested, laughing.

"Yeah. Squishy." We giggled.

I was amazed that I could shift so quickly from sorrow to joy. Maybe it was because of Tally, and being here at Quaker Pines. I didn't want to go home.

10

Home Again

I DID PLAY THE PIANO FOR THE LAST CAMPFIRE SHOW. BUT nobody gathered around me. I played in the background, and sang with the others, the songs that John and I and several other kids had written. The show was a success—not a smashing success like our cabin show, but gently funny—and was followed by a sing-along.

Somehow it didn't matter that I wasn't at the center. As the flames decreased and the logs turned to bright glowing embers, campers came to the forefront, one by one, to express their gratitude for these weeks at Quaker Pines, and to say farewell.

As I listened, I realized that I knew nearly all the kids here by name, and also by some particular trait. There was José Ortega, who had more base hits than any other camper. There was Consuela Vacero, the oldest of ten children, always with some funny story to tell. There was Oscar Riopel, strong and burly, who wouldn't speak to anybody for the whole first week; his father was in prison, we now knew, for he had confessed it tonight by the campfire, his voice barely audible: "I found friends here. People don't hold it against me about my pa bein' in jail. This here is a—a fine place."

It dawned on me then that we were all "special cases," that is, people needing help.

I wanted to speak, but my heart was too full. Had I attempted it, I know I would have cried. And yet I wanted so very much to let Mary know how I felt. I was filled with gratitude and also a sense of obligation. Someday, I thought, I would be the giver, not the recipient. I thought of John's words in the meadow, about making plans, and I whispered a promise to myself: *I will, I will*, though the dream was not entirely clear, not yet.

We sang one last song, my favorite, "One World." I looked around at the faces of my new friends. John was seated on a log, surrounded by boys. Ellen, leading the song, seemed to be singing it directly to him. I wish I could say that my envy was gone, but it wasn't. It lived within me like a deep thorn.

Why had he kissed me? Why had he spent time with me? I felt betrayed and foolish, for while I vowed not to care and not to let him shatter me with his look or his voice, every time I saw John, every time I spoke to him, that pattering, crashing feeling returned; I had it bad, as Tally said. She leaned over to whisper, "I'm so glad we were cabin mates, Annie."

"Me, too," I said. "Maybe we can see each other in the city."

Tally said, "Wouldn't that be fine?"

I said, "You can come over to my house. We can go to

the high school and play tennis, and get an ice cream at the
store near my house.''

"I'd love to see your dog," she said. "Skippy."

Somehow it seemed reasonable that the two worlds, camp
and home, could come together smoothly, without a clash.
Here, as we heard the last strains of the song, "One World,"
it seemed altogether possible.

Our things were packed. We hung around outside our
cabins with our bundles, waiting for the trucks to take us
down to the village.

A boy came running. "Annie! Mary wants to see you in
the office. Right now."

I glanced at my cabin mates, shrugged, and ran off. In
the office Mary sat at her desk, confronting piles of papers,
and when I entered she said, "Annie, something has come
up."

I stopped dead in my tracks. Something at home? Something bad?

Mary continued. "I find, suddenly, that we have a va-
cancy for next session."

"Next session?" I repeated. "I didn't know there was a
next session."

"It's a short session, only twenty-five days. Runs to the
end of August," Mary explained. "I have a number of schol-
arships available to us from various agencies. One of the
campers has caught measles and won't be able to come.
So"—she clasped her hands together and looked at me—"I
wanted to invite you. It would be without any cost to your
parents," she added quickly. "Would you like to come?"

"Me?" I stared at Mary, and my eyes filled with tears. "You want me?"

"Very much," she said. "You could help out with the younger campers. We can't actually make you a junior counselor. You have to be fourteen for that. But maybe by next summer—you could work on it, Annie. I'd love to have you next summer as junior counselor in charge of the horses."

Whatever words I might have said, they slipped away, and I stood there, unable to do anything but nod and say, "Yes, yes, I'll come. Oh, Mary!"

"Next session doesn't start for ten days. Here's all the information," she said. "Have your parents sign the permission forms and mail them back to me."

Finally I was composed enough to ask, "Is anyone else from this session coming back?"

"All the counselors," said Mary. She grinned. "Including John." She gave me a glowing smile, handed me the envelope, and got up. "The trucks are here. Let's go."

The ride home, first on the trucks, then on buses, seemed much shorter. At the midway stop, Tallahassee and I decided to spend the last of our coins on Cokes and candy bars. We lined up at the snack shack. Suddenly, there was Herbie, pulling my arm and looking half away from me, being shy. "Hey," he whispered, "come here a minute."

"I'm in *line*, Herbie," I objected, glancing about.

But he was persistent, pulling my arm and telling me, "I've gotta talk to you. Privately."

It was that last word that did it. Stifling a grin, I gave up my place in line and followed Herbie to a stone bench. "Sit down,'' he said in a very low voice, sneaking glances all around.

I sat.

"I've got something for you," Herbie said with a mysterious little smile. He reached into his pocket, then held out his closed fist.

"What is it, Herbie? Something you made?"

He nodded.

"Let me see it."

Herbie opened his hand. There lay a neckerchief slide made of redwood, patiently carved and sanded.

"Thanks, Herbie!" I exclaimed. "This must have taken hours and hours to make."

"Naw," said Herbie with a shrug. "I love you!" he rattled off, then ran away as if he were being chased by a wild bull.

I smiled to myself and showed Tallahassee the gift.

"I know," she told me. "He's been working on it for the last two weeks. Every day. Hey, if you marry my little brother, we'll be sisters! Wouldn't that be something!" Tallahassee laughed and laughed. It was preposterous, of course—black and white sisters.

Camp had obliterated the barriers for Tallahassee and me.

"Let's not lose track of each other," I said earnestly.

"We'll try," Tally said. "You know, you're the first white girl I could really talk to. Like about boys, and about my cousin Regina."

She had told me about her pale-skinned cousin, Regina, who moved from Atlanta to Chicago to try to "pass" for white. Regina ultimately had a nervous breakdown and tried to commit suicide by cutting her wrists.

"You can't be different from what you are," Tallahassee summed up. "You can't cut out your core, like you was an old apple!"

I knew what she meant. The closer we got toward Los Angeles and home, the more I felt the gradual return of the old Annie, the pulling away from my camp buddies, as if they were already gone. I looked forward to running out into our backyard, sitting up in the olive tree. I was eager to get my skates on and take Skippy for a good run. I couldn't wait to tell Lisa everything I'd done at camp, and to have a piece of Mama's famous pound cake. But part of me wanted to stay away with my new friends. When the bus pulled in at the station I looked and looked, but saw none of my family. Other kids rushed up to their parents, chattering and laughing. I stood alone by the luggage, which had been unloaded into a heap at the side of the bus. I looked over the crowd of parents, sisters, and brothers, and felt a sense of shock and desolation.

Maybe they had forgotten. Maybe there had been an accident. Maybe the whole house had burned down, and I was now alone in the world—it served me right, thinking awful and critical thoughts, wanting to stay with strangers instead of my own, beloved family. . . . I was about to run and find Mary when I heard Papa's voice.

"Annie! Come on! I have the car over there. Where is your suitcase?"

"Papa!" I exclaimed. My father smiled and laid his hand momentarily on my shoulder, then scooped up my bag and nodded for me to take the sleeping bag.

"What's wrong, Papa?" I ran after him. "Why are we in such a hurry? I wanted you to meet some of my friends."

"I'm parked in a bad spot," he said. "And your mother is waiting."

"Where is she? Didn't she come to meet me?"

"Home with Ruth," said my father. "Peter is coming this evening on the train from Michigan. So they are getting ready. Women!" He laughed, but I could see that he was worried about something.

"Peter is coming!" I exclaimed. "Ruth must be so excited."

I imagined how Ruth must feel, her breathless anticipation for tonight. After two years' absence, to see the man she loved! Probably he would give her a ring tonight, a diamond. I was so thrilled for my beautiful sister.

Papa motioned me to the car. "Let's go."

I hung back to look for Tallahassee. I'd wanted to meet her father. With a jolt, I realized that I didn't have Tallahassee's telephone number. How could we get together? I thought again. I'd given her my address and phone number. Okay, I thought, trying to settle down. Don't panic. Keep calm.

"Come on, Annie," Papa prodded me, and we got into the car.

My father lit a cigarette. I saw by the squint of his eyes and the way he tapped his fingers against the steering wheel that he was nervous. It always made him nervous when boys came to the house.

The instant Papa pulled into the driveway, Skippy dashed out to meet me. He leaped up on me, sniffing, wagging, kissing my hands. I held him and kissed him, and then Mama came running out and gave me a huge hug.

"Child! Child! Oh, I think you have grown, let me look

at you. Annie, good heavens, your neck is *black* with dirt. Look at your hands! Didn't they ever let you bathe there?"

Ruth stood at the doorway. Her hair was up in pin curls, and she wore a red bandanna. She waved her arms. "Don't let her bring that filthy suitcase in here! I've just cleaned the whole house."

"Ruth! Ruth!" I called. "When is he coming?"

"I'm not sure," she called back. "He's phoning from Union Station. Annie, please get cleaned up. I don't want him to see you like that."

"What's wrong with me?"

"You're filthy, that's what! Mother, make her get into the tub. And then, scrub it out. Suppose Peter wants to use the bathroom? Oh, Lord, if I only had a place of my own."

"Where's Lisa?" I looked around; I had expected her to come rushing to meet me.

"Out," Papa said curtly.

"Always out with some boy," Mama complained. "It's a wonder she comes home to sleep."

Papa brought my suitcase and sleeping bag into the backyard, where I shook everything out and dumped it into the large laundry basin on the back porch. I pulled off my shoes and socks on the porch, realized that my feet were, indeed, filthy, and hurried into the bathroom for a good soak in the tub.

Mama opened the bathroom door and peered inside. "Annie, be sure to clean the bathtub when you are finished. And put out fresh towels."

"Will you sit with me, Mother? I can't wait to tell you about camp."

"Later we'll have time to talk. I have to get ready. Ruth wants me to change my dress—well, I understand how it is when a girl brings her young man home for the first time." Mama smiled and got that flushed look, as always when romance was in the air.

I settled back in the tub, thinking of Mary, of John, of Tallahassee. Suddenly, I felt lonely here in my own home.

I got out of the tub and dried myself. I brushed my hair until it shone and looked at myself, full-length and clearly. I was tanner. More freckled. There was, too, a different look about me. I looked strong.

After I cleaned the bathroom, I went into the room I shared with Lisa and got dressed in a clean skirt and blouse, then got out my journal. The pages were creased and a bit dirty from travel. I had discontinued my writing at camp, too busy talking to my friends at night, too busy living it. Now I opened it up and wrote: "It feels odd being home again."

The house was silent. Papa was probably outside in the garage, working. Skippy lay on my bed, panting and staring at me. I lay down beside him, held him close to me. He licked my face over and over again.

"You're glad to see me, aren't you?" I murmured. "Let me tell you about camp, Skippy. I met some great kids. . . ."

I kissed and petted him, then got up, went to my desk, and wrote, "The Adventures of Annie Platt, Her Thirteenth Summer, Life at Quaker Pines, and Falling in Love."

We always ate dinner precisely at six.

"Please, let's wait tonight, Papa," Ruth said, her face pale, eyes so bright and flaming that it seemed she must have a fever. "I thought Peter would be here by now. I thought we'd invite him for dinner."

"We have plenty of food, Arthur," Mother added. She looked pretty in a blue-and-white print dress, and she had put on a touch of lipstick.

"Yes, all right," Papa said. "We can wait." He turned to me. "Why don't you play us a tune, Annie? I haven't heard any piano since you left."

Surprised and pleased, I went to the upright piano that stood in a corner of the dining room, opened my songbook, and played "Home on the Range," the family favorite, then "Clementine," which Ruth loved.

We were all singing, even Mama, when Lisa walked in, and in her dramatic way came over to the piano and with her hand on my shoulder, sang harmony.

We sang all the old songs, Papa booming the bass, Mother in her high soprano, and I felt surrounded by love.

Suddenly the telephone rang, breaking the spell.

Mother went to answer; it was for Lisa. Ruth scowled and cried frantically, "Get off the phone! Get off the phone!"

Mama went into the kitchen to get supper, Papa sat down, fork in hand, ready to eat, and he called to Lisa, "It's suppertime! No more telephone talking!"

At last we gathered around the table, and the tension lay over us like a layer of cloud. I thought of camp, of how we sang at the table, and of all the laughter and joking and fun.

This was obviously not the moment to tell about being invited back.

"Well, tell us about camp," Mama said pleasantly enough, and I began, dubiously at first, then animatedly tell-

ing about the cabins, the lake, the horses, the baseball hit I
made, the girls in my cabin, all except for Nancy Rae.

"Tallahassee!" Lisa exclaimed. "What an odd name.
Where's she from?"

"I don't know exactly where she lives," I said with a
shrug. "Somewhere in L.A. But her folks are originally from
Alabama."

Lisa rolled her eyes. "But what kind of people give their
child a name like that?" she scoffed.

"We call her Tally for short," I said. "I think it's a great
name—so unusual and pretty. Like faraway places."

Ruth seemed transported into her own thoughts; she said
nothing during my entire recitation, but sat unblinking, staring into space. She had eaten hardly anything at all.

After the dishes were done we sat in the living room
listening to music from the radio. Mother was busy sewing,
and so was Papa. Lisa did her nails. Ruth pretended to be
reading a magazine, but she looked up every minute or two,
watching the telephone, as if by her will she could make it
ring.

It was nearly ten o'clock. Soon Papa would get up,
stretch, and declare, "It's my bedtime."

The doorbell rang.

Everyone froze. Everyone looked at Ruth.

Skippy barked. I pulled him away from the door, out into
the hallway.

Ruth turned and gave us a look. It said more clearly than
words, *"Scatter!"*

We all got up at once and in our confusion bumped into
one another in the doorway. Lisa and I burst out giggling

and, with our hands over our mouths, ran down the hall into our room, Skippy streaking behind us, and we fell on the beds, giggling.

We soon grew quiet, imagining the encounter of the two young lovers. And then, in accord, Lisa and I opened our bedroom door and sat motionless, listening.

The house was small enough and the walls thin enough so that with some straining, we could hear almost every word. Lisa and I looked at each other in guilty pleasure for eavesdropping, and I held my hand over my mouth so as not to laugh, because once I got the giggles, it was almost impossible to stop.

As the words came clear, and Ruth's voice rose from curiosity to alarm, Lisa and I moved out into the hall, propelled by what we heard.

"You loved me—you said you loved me!"

"The world has changed, Ruth. I'm not the dumb kid I was before. You can't imagine the things I've seen."

"But what has that to do with us? Peter, I waited for you. I never even looked at another man—I love you."

"Look—you're a sweet kid. But we don't want the same things anymore. I can't be part of that old life. . . ."

"But time will change it, Peter! You'll forget."

"No. I'll never forget the things I saw. Piles of bodies. They slaughtered the Jews, in worse ways than we slaughter pigs and cattle. Can you even begin to understand? And the Jews sat there *praying*. Being a Jew only leads to disaster. To death. I'm leaving, Ruth."

"What?" We heard her cry of anguish. "You're leaving the human race? The world? What are you saying?"

"I'm converting. I know you would never do that. I'm joining a church. Changing my name. Getting myself a new life. Away from this—this evil."

"Peter, you can't run away. The world follows you. Give it time. You just got back. . . ."

"At least I came in person to tell you," he said. "I'm leaving again tonight."

"Tonight?"

After a few silent moments, we heard the front door slam.

We waited, unwilling to burst in upon Ruth, unwilling to see her pain.

At last we opened the door to the living room. Ruth was not there. We looked in her room, in the kitchen. Then Papa went outside and I heard him calling her name along the street. "Ruth! Ruth!" His voice was deep and resonant. "Ruth! Ruth!"

Some time later Papa and Ruth came back. Ruth went immediately to her room. Papa's expression was fierce. He looked too angry even to smoke.

He stormed out to the kitchen, and Lisa and I scurried to our room, and he shouted to Mama, his voice thundering through the house, "You see what happens when they take up with strangers?"

Papa raged on and on. "Who was that boy? Who are his people? What do we know about them? Nothing! Nothing! He strings her along for two years, then drops her! Why couldn't she find a boy from here? From the German club? Who said she had to go running around like some cheap tramp, meeting soldiers at the USO, sneaking out behind my back? This is what comes of it. Now he drops her. Drops her flat! If I had seen him, I would have killed him!"

"Arthur, Arthur, for God's sake, stop shouting, the neighbors," Mama tried to pacify him. But Papa was wild.

"Why did you let her go with him? How did it happen?"

"What could I do?" Mama cried. "Young girls meet boys—it's always so. You can't watch them every moment, these are modern times."

"I am not so modern!" Papa shouted. "I will not let them go out again with strangers. You see what happens when they don't listen. What good is a father if he cannot get his daughters properly married?"

I lay in my bed, sick to my stomach.

"Annie," Lisa whispered. "Want to come in my bed?"

"Sure," I whispered, and I crawled over in the dark, and we lay together, our hands touching, and I smelled Lisa's sweet perfume.

"Poor Ruth," I whispered.

"I feel so sorry for her," Lisa whispered back.

I had no idea, then, how this night would have its impact on my own future, too.

II

Moving Out

TWO BUSES TOOK ME TO WILSHIRE BOULEVARD, WHERE LISA worked at the bank. The broad boulevard was lined with fashionable shops. I was always a little awed when I entered the high-ceiling bank building with its dark, shining linoleum floors and polished furnishings. As secretary to the assistant manager, Lisa had her own desk and telephone. Beautiful, efficient, and soft-spoken, she seemed no longer my sister, but an important lady with an impressive position.

I walked up, feeling awkward, and Lisa motioned for me to sit down on the chair by her desk. "I have to stamp these letters," she said. "Then we can go."

She had a little contraption that rolled water onto the stamps, and she stamped those letters, sealed them, gathered them up along with her purse and sweater; everything she did was sleek and professional. How I admired her! Lisa was poised, beautiful, competent. And she brought home a nice paycheck every two weeks.

We walked out and down the boulevard to a lunchroom,

where we ordered our usual. Lisa had a chicken salad sandwich and I had grilled cheese. Even our choice of foods, I
thought, signified our differences; Lisa was elegant with her
chicken salad, I was plain and simple with my cheese.

"So, what's wrong?" Lisa asked after several minutes.

I glanced up sharply. "Who said anything's wrong?"

"You've been remarkably silent," said Lisa. "So something must be bothering you."

"I met a boy," I said, blurting it out. "John Wright.
He's absolutely wonderful."

Lisa smiled and chewed daintily on her chicken salad
sandwich. She wiped her lips carefully. "Did he kiss you?"

"Yes."

"Did you like it?"

"Yes. But I'm confused."

Lisa laughed. "Welcome to the club!" she exclaimed.

"What club?"

"The love club," she said. "The club of confusion. Tell
me about him."

And she listened, nodding and smiling while I told her
everything about John. "He's so clever and talented. We
planned the last campfire show. He wrote most of the songs.
I played the piano and we had a sing-along. It was so fabulous. He's seventeen."

"Uh-oh," Lisa said, with a dark frown. "Honey, chalk
it up as just a summer romance," she said. "You're back
home now. You won't be seeing him again."

"But I will," I said eagerly, "if I can go back to camp."
Then I told her about Mary's invitation. "Next year I'd be a
junior counselor," I said breathlessly, "which means I'd go
free and even earn my own spending money. I'd be in charge

of the horses—the horses, Lisa! I learned to groom and saddle them. You can't imagine how wonderful it is to ride. Oh, Lisa, it's so beautiful there in the mountains. In the morning, first thing, you smell the pine trees and you hear that stillness; it's heaven.''

Lisa nodded, a faraway look in her eyes. She murmured, ''You always were different. You know, willing to take chances. You're not afraid to try new things.''

I paused. It was true. I was always the one reaching out for new experiences, finding new friends. I glanced at Lisa and saw her wistful look. I felt equal to her, suddenly, and very capable.

''Quaker Pines is the best place in the world,'' I went on. ''Nobody makes you feel poor. They talk about love and wonderful things, about brotherhood and one world. You know, everyone is alike under the skin. There's something else I need to tell you. About my cabin mate, Tallahassee.''

''What about her?''

''She's a Negro.''

Lisa gazed at me. She flushed. ''It figures,'' she said.

''What do you mean?''

''You're that way. You'll do anything. I—you feel okay with people who are so different. I never know what to say.''

''That's the point,'' I said. ''They aren't different.''

''Well.'' Lisa waved me aside. ''You were lucky. Quaker Pines sounds like a great place.'' She stirred sugar into her coffee, looking thoughtful and sad.

I said, ''I want to go back. More than anything. Would you talk to them for me?''

Lisa sighed. ''I don't think I have much influence now. They're mad at me. Especially Mother.''

"Why? What happened?"

"Just the usual yelling and screaming and restrictions and rules—enough to drive a person crazy. Every time I buy a new dress, Mother makes me feel guilty. Every time a boy calls, Papa acts like I'm a tramp. What do they want from me? To join a nunnery?"

I shook my head. "You'd make a terrible nun, Lisa."

We both burst out laughing so hard that tears ran down our faces, and people turned to stare.

"Okay, Annie," Lisa said, wiping her eyes with her napkin, composing herself. "I'll try to talk to them. Trouble is, Papa's upset with me, too."

"Why?"

"I broke up with Nate."

"Why would he be angry about that?"

"He doesn't like me going out with different boys." She sighed. "He thinks it's cheap. He'd rather I'd be tied to one man for the rest of my life, just to make him feel secure. Well, I won't do it!" she said, thrusting out her chin in defiance.

"I thought you loved Nate."

Suddenly she began to cry, dabbing her eyes with the edge of her napkin. I always hated to see my sister cry; her eyes filled, tears overflowed, her lips became full and puffed.

"What is it?" I whispered, leaning toward her.

"He's hateful and mean!" Lisa sobbed. "He doesn't want to get married. He doesn't want to be tied down, he says."

"Then you can go on the road," I exclaimed. "You don't have to make the choice. You always wanted to dance, all your life, Lisa! Why don't you do it?"

Lisa shifted in her chair, dried her eyes, and suddenly called for our check. "You don't understand," she said, her tone cold.

"What's there to understand? You have a chance to go on the stage. Maybe you'll be famous, like Ginger Rogers or Ann Miller."

"Annie, Annie," she said, almost laughing, "I'm not talented like those women! All I'd be is in the chorus in some awful, dingy summer stock theater."

"Well, I'll bet Ann Miller and Ginger Rogers began that way," I said stoutly. "You could be discovered, Lisa. There are always producers at those shows. I know, I read all the movie magazines. And if you don't try, Lisa, you'll never know. All your life you'll wonder whether you might have become—"

"Oh, Annie, what do you know about it?" Lisa snapped. "If I leave now, Nate is going to find someone else for sure. I've invested three years in this relationship. Why should I just walk away from it?"

"But you're walking away from dancing, from being on your own. . . ."

"On my own?" she said, her voice low, but filled with rage. "Why do I want to be on my own? I want to get married! I want a house and babies, someone taking care of me. Why not? Ever since I was twelve years old I had to clean the house and cook meals and sew for Papa and take care of you. Mama was never home, they were always working. I'm tired! It's time for somebody to take care of me for a change."

I was stunned. I felt sick, pushing aside the rest of my grilled cheese sandwich. I didn't even have the appetite for the sour pickle, which I usually saved for the end.

Tears filled my eyes, heavy tears of loss and also shame. All these years I had been a burden to my sister. All those times she took me along to see her friends, to the movies, or the beach, she had resented it.

She must have read my thoughts, for Lisa got up and came to me, laid her hand on my shoulder. "Honey, I didn't mean . . ."

"It's okay," I said, looking away. "Let's go. You'll be late for work."

I walked Lisa back to the bank, and then for a long, long time I walked along Wilshire Boulevard, rather than catching the bus. I wanted to walk forever, to lose myself among all these people, strangers and unpredictable; but at least, I thought, they couldn't hurt me.

For the next few days I applied myself to making money. My best source was Papa. He paid a dollar a collar; it was a slogan in our house. He bought the beautiful fox fur collars. We sewed in the satin lining, using tiny, almost invisible stitches. It was painstaking work. One collar took me nearly an hour. If I was industrious, I could sew four, maybe even five in a day.

That Friday night I had a baby-sitting job next door. During dinner I kept looking at Lisa, nudging her under the table; she had agreed to steer the conversation toward growing up and new experiences and opportunities, ending of course in her plea that I be allowed to return to Quaker Pines.

It began well enough, as Papa innocently announced, "Annie has helped me so much this week. She earned eighteen dollars sewing collars. A dollar a collar," he said with a smile and a flourish. "You did a good job," he added.

"Thank you, Papa." I smiled happily. "It's always good to have a skill," I added, parroting Papa's own advice.

"Oh, yes," Lisa quickly agreed. "At camp Annie learned to take care of horses, didn't you, Annie?"

Papa laughed. "Not many horses to take care of around here!"

"She also waited on tables, didn't you, Annie?"

"Yes," I said. "We take turns. And we do KP. And I helped take care of Mary's little girl. I learned a lot of skills at camp."

"You didn't learn to make your bed," Mother said rather sharply.

I caught my breath, aghast at this betrayal. It was true; I usually didn't make my bed until Mother nagged and nagged. Still, I wanted Papa to count my virtues, not my faults.

I screwed up my courage and began bravely, rather loudly, "Mary, the codirector, says that I—"

My old enemy, the telephone, intervened.

Papa leaped up to answer it, held out the receiver to Lisa. "For you," he said abruptly.

The telephone table stood only a few feet from our dining table, so we all heard Lisa's responses.

"Well, yes. When, did you say? That's a little sooner than I had expected—oh. Well, that could work out. Furnished? Yes, yes. Of course. Great. I do love the place. Thank you. Thank you for calling. Yes. And thank you, Mrs. Sherwin! Good-bye."

Lisa came back to the table, walking with her head high. On her cheeks were two bright spots of color. As she picked up her glass, I noticed that her hand shook slightly.

"So, what was that about?" Papa asked. "Why do your

friends always call at dinnertime? Don't they have any respect for family?''

"It wasn't a friend," Lisa said. "Just an—associate.''

"Ah, an associate," said Mama, her eyes glittering. "She doesn't have friends. Our Lisa is getting high up in the business world with *associates*.''

I knew that the struggle between them lay much deeper than the telephone call. Lisa and Mama didn't see eye to eye on many things. Lisa loved to spend money; Mother always wanted to save. Lisa longed for improvements; Mother thought we ought to be satisfied with our lot. On and on and on; they were nearly always at odds.

I bit my lip, realizing I should have dealt with my camp problem alone. I'd already been home for four days. I needed to get that permission slip signed, but I was terribly afraid of being refused.

Lisa finished her water. She put down her napkin, looked from Papa to Mother, and said, "That was a lady called Mrs. Sherwin. She has an apartment for rent on Crescent Street, near Wilshire, not far from the bank. I went to see the apartment last week and she said she wanted to check with my employer. She is satisfied now that I'll be a good tenant. I'm moving out tomorrow.''

It was like an eclipse or a thunderbolt. Nobody moved. Mama gripped the edge of the table. I could feel my heart thumping. And Papa—his mouth dropped, his face became bleached of color, and he turned in his chair, his expression terrible.

I was afraid. Once, he had whipped Ruth with a stick—I don't remember why. A long time ago he had spanked me for running across the street to the fish wagon. But more than being hit, I was afraid of his wrath, the way he would shout and pursue the wrongdoer, relentless and fearsome.

Nothing changed for a full minute. Then Papa said, "So this is the new country. When young girls leave their father's protection and their mother's love. This is the great America?"

He threw down his napkin and scraped back his chair, and we heard him walking through the back of the house out to his sanctuary, his workshop in the garage.

Mother's eyes were red rimmed. "You have hurt him very deeply," she said to Lisa. "Someday, when you have children of your own—"

"Oh, stop it, Mother!" Lisa cried. "Stop trying to make me feel guilty. I'm sick and tired of being treated like a child. I'm sick and tired of being made to feel guilty because I want the same things all normal girls want—you're always complaining about me. Now you can be happy. I'll be out of your way."

Lisa stormed out and went to our room. I started to follow, but Mother called me back: "The dishes, Annie. Don't think I'm going to do these by myself."

The dishes, the damn dishes! I wanted to scream. Always, dishes came before personal disasters. I heaped the plates high, carried them into the kitchen, turned on the water in a furious, fast stream, and sent the suds flying while I scraped and washed.

Leaving! Lisa was leaving, and I'd be here alone. How could she do this to me? And she hadn't even told me.

The phone rang again. Mrs. Schatz from next door wanted me to come over immediately. I rushed into our bedroom, where Lisa was packing her sweaters and skirts into a large cardboard box.

"Lisa, I have to go baby-sit, but I . . ."

"Go on, then."

"I need to talk to you. Lisa . . ."

"We'll talk another time. I'm sorry about your camp thing. I couldn't help it. But after all, I have to take care of my own problems."

It felt like a door being slammed. "But—when will I see you? When will we talk again? If you're leaving tomorrow . . ."

Lisa came to me, drew near, and I smelled the sweetness of her perfume and felt the softness of her cheek. "Annie, we'll always be sisters. I'll call you from the bank. We'll have lunch. And as soon as I get settled in my new place, I'll have you over."

"But it won't be the same," I protested. "We've always slept together. I'll be all alone."

"You'll have the room to yourself," Lisa said. "You can put up any pictures you want. You can have all the dresser drawers and the whole closet."

"I don't want those," I cried. "I want *you*."

But she put me off firmly, saying, "I'm sorry, Annie. We all have to grow up. I have to do this. Someday you'll be in my place. You'll understand."

Mother yelled to me from the kitchen. "Annie! Mrs. Schatz is *here* at the door. She wants you to come over *now*, what's the matter with you?"

I grabbed a book and a couple of fur collars and linings and ran next door.

For the next five hours I was busy feeding and playing with those kids. After they went to bed I turned on the radio, softly, and listened to music while I stitched three more collars.

I'd start taking care of myself, I decided. Earn money. Learn skills. Get ready to make it on my own.

The Schatzes didn't come home until two in the morning. They paid me three dollars, including a tip, and I had earned three more dollars sewing. But I was exhausted and miserable, and the next morning when I heard Lisa rummaging around I pulled the pillow over my ears and dived down under the blankets.

When I woke up again it was eleven o'clock in the morning. Lisa was gone. Even the blankets were gone from her bed. And somebody was ringing the doorbell nonstop, yelling my name.

I gasped, grabbed my jeans, jumped into them fast. I knew that voice! It was Tallahassee, here at my front door.

12

A Missing Person

I FLUNG OPEN THE DOOR, AND THERE STOOD TALLAHASSEE, big as life and all smiles. When I say big as life I mean I had forgotten how tall Tallahassee was. At camp, among the trees and open spaces, she seemed to fit quite handily. Here, standing on my front porch, Tallahassee looked enormous, and her grin was the biggest, widest I had ever seen.

"Hey! Bet you're surprised to see me! How've you been? My daddy was coming across town and I told him, 'Daddy, drop me off at my friend's house.' He'll meet me back here later, okay? I've got all day. Daddy works till five today, which is tons of time—aren't you going to ask me in?"

"Of course, come in!" I drew Tally inside and gave her a big hug. "Oh, I sure missed you," I exclaimed. "Come on into my room."

Skippy bounded in. Tally bent to embrace him. We went to my room and sat on the bed, Tally patting and crooning to Skippy as if they had known each other forever.

"I love your room," Tallahassee exclaimed. "It's so

pretty. And you have two windows! You can see the backyard from here. And two beds! You can have friends sleep over, can't you?''

"That's true," I said. "My sister just moved out. I suppose I can have friends over now. Except that . . ." I'd never had anybody sleep over. Somehow, our family didn't seem the type.

"Where'd your sister go?"

"To live in an apartment. She didn't like my dad bossing her around."

"Just like my stepmom," said Tally with a grin. "She left us a couple of weeks ago. Said she couldn't stand all the kids."

"Where's Herbie?"

"Oh, he's staying with my aunt. They've got two other boys, so he'll have company. I'm trying to get a job," said Tally, her face suddenly serious. "I've got to make me some money, or I won't even have gym clothes for school."

"I've been trying to make money, too," I said. "For camp."

"Hey! Are you going back?"

"I haven't really asked them yet," I explained, and told Tally everything that had happened—Ruth's breakup with Peter, Lisa moving out. "My folks don't like to deal with more than one calamity at a time," I said, laughing. Having a friend to share things with made my troubles seem much smaller.

Tally glanced over at my piggy bank, really a large mayonnaise jar with some coins and a few bills stuffed into it. She asked, "Do you have a job now?"

"I baby-sit sometimes, and I sew for my father," I replied.

"Boy, you're lucky," Tally said. She looked around my room, then said, "I can do real nice little stitches. Do you think your father would let me work for him?"

I eyed her dubiously. "I don't know, Tally. Up till now, Papa hasn't hired anybody but us."

"Maybe I could see what you do," she said. "Maybe you'd teach me."

"I suppose I could," I said, nodding slowly. It seemed like a good idea. Papa was always looking for help. "Sure," I said with enthusiasm. "I could teach you what to do."

I ran to the living room closet, where a box of fur collars and linings always stood ready, just in case any of us had some extra time and the desire to "sew a collar, earn a dollar."

I scooped up the collar, lining, thread, and needle and rushed back to show Tallahassee.

She bent close to me in concentration as I showed her how to turn under the hem of the lining, how to start the stitches so that the knot wouldn't show, how to push the needle through the tough hide with a thimble, making tiny, almost invisible stitches.

"Whew," Tally sighed, shaking her head. "You're good. I guess I could learn. Can I try it?"

I handed Tally the fur collar and the needle. She fumbled with the needle, dropped it, rethreaded it, bent to her task, the tip of her tongue tucked tightly between her teeth.

Suddenly my stomach rumbled. Tally and I both laughed.

"You're hungry," Tally said. "Haven't you had breakfast?"

"No. I just woke up when you came," I said. "Let's go fix some eggs. Are you hungry?"

"I sure could eat," Tallahassee said.

We went into the kitchen and I broke open four eggs, got out some bread for toast, and milk for hot chocolate.

"Where's your folks?" Tally asked as we sat in the kitchen alcove eating.

"My mom's at work with that baby I told you about. My dad's usually out back in the garage or else downtown selling his coats. Probably downtown now." Then I remembered. "Oh! Papa told me yesterday he had to go down to the motor vehicle place. He needs to get a new driver's license." It was not a good time to ask him about camp, so I had waited again.

"I sure hope he passes the test," I added.

Tally sympathized. "Adults hate that stuff—turns them into grizzly bears when they have to go downtown to some office. You're best off to get out of here."

"Where do you want to go?" I asked.

"How about taking the bus down to the beach?" Tally suggested.

I paused, reluctant. "I've never gone to the beach alone," I said.

"You wouldn't be alone. You'd be with me."

"I mean, I usually go with my sister. I don't know. . . ."

Tallahassee shrugged. "If you don't want to, it's okay," she said. "I've got carfare, though," she added. "And we could get us some cotton candy. And ride the Ferris wheel."

"I love the Ferris wheel!" I cried.

"Come on then!"

I quickly pulled the bedspread over my bed, then rinsed off our dishes and stacked them neatly in the sink. I remembered the frying pan, filled it with suds to soak, wiped the table and counters, and scribbled a note to my mother and propped it up on the kitchen table.

"I'll be back by four," it said. "My camp friend came. We took the bus to the beach. Love, Annie."

In my room I took a dollar and twenty cents out of the glass jar, and with the coins jingling in my pocket, I set out happily with Tally to walk the five blocks up to Wilshire Boulevard. There we caught the bus that went all the way out to the beach.

Even the long bus ride was better than I ever remembered it, because Tally could make me laugh at anything. She'd point at a store window or a passerby, then launch into some comic tale, until the two of us were bent over giggling, and I was having the best time of my life. Free! I thought as the bus sped along the street. I saw everything with new eyes: the tall, bending palm trees, the clean, sleek buildings, the bustling people. How good it felt not to be the little sister tagalong, but to go on my own with a friend. At last the bus, hissing and groaning, heaved its way down the steep ramp to the Santa Monica exit, and with two blasts of the horn the driver called out, "Last Stop! Santa Monica Beach."

Tally and I raced down the ramp to the sand. Laughing, we pulled off our shoes and socks, then ran to the water's edge. We rolled up our pants and went in up to our knees, and we ran, squealing like little kids, when the big waves rolled in to the shore. Of course, our pants got soaked, but then we lay in the sand to dry, and we talked and giggled and had the best time in the world.

We rode the Ferris wheel twice, clutching each other and screaming. We ate cotton candy and hot dogs and chips, and because we were running out of money we shared an ice-cream sandwich.

A woman came by with her husband; the two leaned together like bent twigs. The woman bobbed her head, pointed a sharp finger, and rasped out at me, "You better behave yourself, young lady! You better go home. What are you, a juvenile delinquent?"

I was so shocked I couldn't say a word.

Tally grabbed my arm and we raced off down the pier. "What a priss-puss." Tally giggled.

Inside, I seethed. "How dare that woman talk to me like that!"

"My daddy says people like that probably got a bum break themselves. It makes 'em mean."

"Like Nancy Rae," I said.

"Yeah."

"You've had some bum breaks," I remarked. "You're not mean."

"Oho!" called out Tally, making a fist and a terrible face. "You should see me in my mean streak! My daddy says I'm a devil on wheels. Hey—it's after three," she said, "we better get going."

"After three! Oh murder, it takes at least an hour to get home, and I said four o'clock."

"What's a few minutes?" Tally asked, and all the way home on the bus, while I fretted about the time, Tally soothed me. "Maybe your folks aren't even home yet, Annie. You left a note. You cleaned up your stuff. They won't care."

"You don't know my folks," I said gloomily. "They never want me to do anything. They don't want me to grow up."

"Parents are like that," Tally said sympathetically. Then she added, "I wouldn't know for myself, but I hear it."

I sighed, wondering which of us was worse off.

To my vast relief we arrived at our stop on Wilshire at five minutes to four. Whooping with delight, our towels streaming behind us, Tally and I raced down the last five blocks to my house, and we landed on the porch, laughing and panting, and just as I put my hand out to press the bell, the door flew open and my mother stood there, her face a vision of fury.

"Annie," she cried. She pulled me in. My father appeared behind her, holding the long bamboo rod with which he flogged the fur collars to puff them up. He shouted out, "She's here? She's here? Wait until I finish with her."

"Arthur, no." My mother pushed him.

Amid the commotion I became aware of Tally's gasp and her wide-eyed stare, and I called out, "Mother, Mother, what's wrong? I left a note. I was at the beach."

My father pushed me aside. He prodded Tallahassee in the shoulder, roughly, as if she were some gigantic dog that stood in our doorway, blocking the light. "Who are you? What are you doing with Annie. How can you come here?"

"Papa," I shouted, tugging at his arm, "this is my camp friend, Tallahassee, she came to see me."

"Who said you could have company?" my mother demanded. "You ate four eggs. Four! How could you eat four eggs? That's a whole week's ration."

"Who cares about eggs?" my father yelled. "What about my fur collars?"

"I was showing Tally—"

"Fur collars all over the living room!" my father shouted. "I thought there was a burglar."

"But—but . . ." Oh, murder, I thought. Skippy. I could just see him seizing those collars and shaking them in his mouth, like prey. Dogs will be dogs. "Skippy must have gotten them out," I said. "I must have forgotten to shut the closet door."

"But I have told you a thousand times," roared my father. "There were fur collars all over the house!"

"Who said you could go to the beach?" my mother demanded. "Since when do you think you can do anything you please, like a juvenile delinquent; don't you ask permission anymore? Is this what they teach at this camp?"

Juvenile delinquent—the words rang back at me from that hateful woman at the beach, and I felt a terrible revulsion at what was happening here, especially with Tally standing beside me on the porch.

"You better go now," my mother scolded Tally, pointing her finger. "You go on home."

"Mother!" I cried, aghast at this rudeness. "Her father's coming. . . ."

Tally said, "Don't worry, Annie. I'll wait at the market. Don't worry. I'll be fine."

"Tally!" I cried. Through a haze of tears I saw Tally hurry away.

Papa lifted his hand as if to strike me. The rod shook in his hand. "Go to your room!" he said.

My room seemed suddenly a box, a prison. Even Skippy had run, whimpering, out to the yard, and I was utterly alone. This is the way the world is, I thought bitterly. Nobody cares. From my room I heard them arguing about me. About Tally.

And the things they said were almost unbelievable, especially coming from my own parents.

"Where does she get these people?"

"She is worse than before—you see what happens. That camp. Strange people. Strange ideas."

"A nigger. *A nigger!*"

The word reverberated in my ears. How could they have used that horrible word? My own parents? How could they? For hours I sat on my bed. I tried to make sense of it. They had been worried. Always imagining the worst, they probably thought I'd been kidnapped. Didn't see my note. Got frantic. Overprotective. All right; I could understand that. But to send Tally away like that! To treat a guest of mine like some horrible criminal, and to call her those awful names, just because her skin was dark . . . I couldn't bear it. I went out to tell them.

At first I argued. I yelled. "I was so ashamed! How could you be so mean to my friend? How could you be so rude?"

"She was the rude one," Mother said. "Was she invited? Did you invite her here?"

"No! She happened to get a ride, and we're friends."

"People don't just drop in like that," Mother said flatly. "Not people with manners and proper upbringing. What kind of a girl can that be? Where does she live? Doesn't anybody teach her anything?"

"She's a wonderful girl!" I defended my friend. "She takes care of her little brother. She's funny and smart and a wonderful friend, and I love her!"

"You love her?" My father seemed about to explode. "Are you crazy? You love a *schwartze*."

"What's the difference what color she is!" I screamed,

unable to stop now. "You are bigoted. You are just like all those people they talked about at camp. You are prejudiced. You are just like the Nazis. This is why there are wars!" I cried. "Because people hate for no reason—how could you?"

"How dare you!" My mother aimed for my cheek. I turned. Her hand came down on the side of my head once, then again. It was not a heavy blow, but I felt her fury.

I sat in my room, unable to sleep throughout the night. I watched the sky turn from deep blue to black. Perhaps I dozed; I don't know. Skippy came scratching at the door. I let him in, pulled him onto my pillow. Even Skippy's warm presence could not subdue the ache in me.

It was still dark when I got out of bed and packed my jeans, a couple of shirts, my swimsuit, and some underwear in my duffel bag. I took eight dollars, which was most of the money from my bank, and stuffed it into the pockets of my jeans. Then I wrote a note in large, conspicuous letters.

DEAR MOTHER AND FATHER,
    I HAVE GONE TO CAMP. I WAS INVITED TO RETURN. IT WILL COST YOU NOTHING. I WILL BE BACK THE END OF AUGUST. DON'T WORRY ABOUT ME, BECAUSE I CAN TAKE CARE OF MYSELF.

I hesitated over the ending. Should I say "love"? What I felt now was pure, white anger.

Hastily I scribbled the two final words—LOVE, ANNIE; then I put the note in the middle of the kitchen table, under the sugar bowl, and crept out the door. I ran with my heavy bag to the corner and, to my delight, saw the bus coming down the street.

I climbed aboard, went clear to the back, and sat watching the houses whiz past. Above the row of seats hung printed advertisements. One was a photograph of a woman with the words underneath, MISSING PERSON, and a description.

I stared at the words. MISSING PERSON.

That's me, I thought. A missing person. I looked around at the other passengers. I stared at the woman in the photograph, and I understood her need to escape; I understood her perfectly.

That woman, like me, needed to be free.

13

On My Own

THINGS LOOK ENTIRELY DIFFERENT WHEN YOU ARE ON YOUR own. More real. Edges are sharper, noises are louder. I was not afraid, but cautious.

At last the bus swung into the large yard outside the Greyhound depot. I got out, pulling my bag behind me.

I had been inside this depot only once before, years ago, when we moved from New York to Los Angeles. I recalled the awful trip, the smell of the exhaust, the long, long days of idle reflection while we crossed the country to California. Now, I was striking out again, this time alone.

Dark benches stood in the dim station room, some filled with people waiting to travel, others just hanging around. I walked up to the huge board where times and destinations were written in bold black letters. I knew I had to get to San Jacinto. From there, I'd have to rely on my luck in finding Ed at the village, or I'd phone him at camp and ask him to come for me. I saw that the next bus was leaving in fifteen minutes.

The woman selling tickets didn't even look up from the book she was reading. "Where ya wanna go?" she asked, disinterested.

"San Jacinto," I said.

"A dollar ten," she said. She pulled off a ticket and handed it to me with hardly a glance.

I had imagined that someone would stop me and ask, "Where're you going, sister?" Or perhaps they would inquire, "You got problems, girlie? You running away?"

But nobody cared. I sat down and realized I was very hungry, having eaten nothing the night before. Well, I had money in my pocket, certainly enough for breakfast, and for a moment I felt proudly independent, having managed to provide for myself. A snack machine stood against the wall. For five cents I bought a bag of potato chips, and for another nickel a cup of hot chocolate.

I sat down and ate the chips greedily. As I brought the hot cocoa to my lips, I saw a man staring at me. He wore a sweatshirt under a jacket, a scarf around his neck, and a battered hat on his head. All his possessions, I knew, were on his body, or in the bulging shopping bag that he carried over his left arm. His right hand lay pressed against his chest, useless, I supposed, from palsy or some accident.

He stared at me.

I looked away.

I finished my chocolate and tossed the cup into a waste can.

Then I dug into my pocket, and purposefully I took out a dime, placed it on the little ledge of the snack machine, and walked away.

I went in again. The man was gone. I glanced to the

ledge. The dime was gone, too. Maybe he was a wino, I thought, and would use my money to get drunk. I sighed.

I thought of calling home to hear my mother's voice and to tell her personally that I was all right. Then I remembered the ugly words and phrases from last night, and I stiffened again in anger. No. Forget it.

The Greyhound bus pulled in exactly on time; I got in line, along with ten or twelve other travelers, then walked again to my favorite spot in the very back of the bus.

With a wide turn and a sharp blast of the horn, the Greyhound left the yard and sped through the streets. I began to nod and soon fell asleep.

I had been dreaming and was entirely oblivious of my surroundings when I awakened. I was sweating from the heat, nauseated by the stench of the bus, and groggy with sleep.

"San Jacinto," the driver called again.

I grabbed my bag and hurried out of the bus.

The little station quickly emptied; a bare bench along the roadway looked hot and dusty, and nothing stirred for as far as I could see. The bus station, obviously, was some distance from the town, with only a shed for shelter, a drink machine standing out on the porch, and that single, solitary bench.

I reached into my pocket and counted my money. Enough to go straight back home. I stood in the roadway, pondering. I felt like a puppet, hanging limp, with nobody to pull its strings and make it move, nobody to decide.

An alley cat darted past me. I reached out; it fled. Nobody trusts anybody, I thought. Nobody cares.

I thought of Mary, the oasis of her cabin, her gentle face and soft voice.

I went to the telephone and dialed the camp number, which was printed at the bottom of the permission slip I had never gotten signed. Now, using a stubby pencil, I scrawled the name, Margo Platt, and wondered what I would tell Mary.

I had not thought about it before. Would I tell the truth? Create a lie? My head spun in confusion, and as I stood there struggling, I heard Sal's voice: "Quaker Pines Camp!"

"Sal!" I shouted into the receiver. "It's Annie. I'm at the bus stop. Is Ed coming to the village today?"

There was a pause, a shuffling sound. Then Sal said brightly, "He sure is, honey. You wait right there. He'll be there within an hour. Just sit tight inside the station house, okay?"

"Okay," I said.

"Promise you won't leave," Sal said.

"Okay," I said.

I went inside and sat down on an old, cane-backed chair. The clerk glanced up dourly; he muttered, " 'lo," and that was the end of our conversation. Whatever he was doing, it involved total concentration and a great deal of newspaper rustling; I glanced up once and saw that he was reading the racing form. Horses. Races.

I thought of Molly and the other horses, the peaceful mountains, the kind people at Quaker Pines, and I waited and waited until finally the door swung open, and there was Ed to drive me, in the battered old truck, up the mountain to camp.

On the way, conversation was casual and easy. "So, you decided to come back," Ed said. "Well, Molly will be glad, you can be sure. She misses the kids. So do all the animals. The kittens have their eyes wide open. They're

racing through the barn and up along the rafters, you should
see 'em!''

"How's Mary?" I asked.

"Mary is all right," said Ed. "A bit tired," he added,
then sighed.

Camp without campers is a strange place, too quiet, dry,
baking in the heat, a ghost town. We pulled up at the flagpole.
Even the flag was missing. Dust billowed up all around us.
The lake was silent; only the squirrels still leaped between
the branches, and from the stable I heard a faint whinny.

Ed opened the trunk and brought out my duffel bag.
"Let's go on up to the office," he said.

Suddenly I was scared. Maybe my parents had called Sal.
Maybe the sheriff was on the way to bring me back in dis-
grace. Or maybe my parents never saw the note, as before,
and had called the police, and they were searching for me.
I had heard stories about runaways and their punishments;
sometimes they are taken away from their parents, classified
as "uncontrollable," sent to detention homes, juvenile hall.
I had read about such things. I felt ill.

In the office, Sal looked up from her desk as if I had never
been gone. "Hello, Annie," she said casually. "I'll give
Mary a call at the cabin."

Ed shuffled off, and I sat down.

I wished Sal would offer me something to drink, even
water. But she was typing busily. The telephone rang. She
answered, rapped out replies to questions about camp. She
hung up, sighed, shook her head at me. "It's always like this
between sessions," she said. "A madhouse. Kitchen help to
find, counselors cancel, others apply, campers, too, supplies

must be bought and stored, poor Ed. He's been running night and day. Douglas is in Riverside buying wholesale meat and groceries. The cook quit. What next?''

In walked Mary, looking, for the first time, worn out and tense. "Annie!" She held out her hand. I went to her. "It's good to see you. You have no idea how good. I'm quite stranded here, with Sal needed on the telephone, Douglas gone—oh, but you wouldn't know what's been going on. Alice has the chicken pox. Have you had chicken pox?''

I nodded, and rapidly Mary continued, "Good, good. Then you can go to her. Beatrice is gone, visiting her people in New Mexico, and Ellen, poor child, is in the infirmary; I need another pair of hands. It's absolutely providential that you've come—if you don't mind, go straight to the infirmary, you can bunk there with Ellen, and see what you can do to make her comfortable. I have to go to town; I simply must go today. While I'm gone, you could stay with Alice. Do you mind?'' Mary smiled at me now for the first time, pushing back the strands of her hair and sighing.

"Of course I don't mind," I said. I had expected quite a different reception—amazement, surprise, stern lectures, even dire punishment. Instead, everybody was frantically busy. Nobody seemed to realize what I had risked to come here, nobody seemed to care about my problems at home.

"I have no help in the kitchen," Mary went on. "Ordinarily we have a cook staying on between sessions. I don't mind cooking for everyone, but with Alice in bed and Ellen in the infirmary . . .'' Mary wrung her hands.

"What's wrong with Ellen?''

"Chicken pox. Same as Alice. She never had it as a child.

I can't keep her with Alice, because she's simply too ill, running a fever. Poor Ellen. We had it all planned, that she'd stay at Quaker Pines between sessions to help me. Then she got this; apparently one of her campers came down with chicken pox the last morning, but we didn't know at the time. I wonder how many other campers from last session will get it. Oh, dear, the phone never stops ringing. We've had to notify all the parents, send letters . . . dear me.''

My stomach rumbled loudly. I said, "May I go to the kitchen and get something to eat?''

"Of course, dear,'' said Mary. "Help yourself to some bread and peanut butter and jam. Perhaps you'd make a sandwich for Ellen, too, she hasn't had a thing but tea all day.''

I turned to go.

"Annie!'' Mary called me back. "Your mother called. She told me you were on the way. I'll telephone her and tell her you arrived safely.''

I heard Mary giving my number to the operator. It was a strange feeling, being connected by that telephone cord, yet separate now, for I had separated myself by running off, by not staying to face my parents. I felt like an outsider listening to a private conversation.

"Oh yes, Mrs. Platt, she's fine. I do need her terribly, and she's going right off to the infirmary to take care of that sick girl. Oh yes, I'll tell her. Good-bye.''

I was stunned. No request that I come to the telephone? I expected Mama to wail and cry, "Annie, how could you? I was so worried. I thought I'd have a heart attack!''

"Didn't she want to talk to me?'' I asked.

"I suppose she did, but she said she had to get to work.

You can write your parents a note when you have time. Now, I really must get back to Alice.''

The kitchen looked huge and forbidding, without anyone in it. The vast, stainless-steel countertops, the deep sinks, the twelve-burner stove, and the huge ovens stood mute and cold and desolate. I tiptoed over to the pantry, opened the huge door, pulled the cord for light, and confronted the shelves filled with groceries. Eventually I found a big jar of peanut butter and another of apple butter. In one of the refrigerators I found several loaves of bread. At last I finished making the sandwiches and wiping up the counter. I put away the food just as I'd found it, wrapped the sandwiches in several napkins, and went out to the infirmary.

I pushed open the door with my foot.

A cloud of stale, heavy air greeted me. Inside, I saw that the windows were all darkened with drapery. I heard a moan.

"Ellen!" I called. "It's me, Annie. Are you awake?"

"Barely," she said, with a groan.

"I brought you something to eat," I said.

"No."

"Mary said you should eat. I made sandwiches."

I put the sandwiches down on the table, went to the window, and drew aside the drape. Now I could see Ellen, her body bunched up under the covers, head down.

"Hi," I said, "I'm sorry you're sick."

"You and me both," mumbled Ellen.

She sat up, propped on her elbow, and I saw her face and nearly gasped. Hives and blisters covered her entire face, and her eyes looked sunken from fever. She looked terrible, her hair matted and dry, her cheeks swollen from the pox.

"I feel as if I've been hit by a truck," she said.

"Who's been taking care of you?" I asked.

"Mary. And Sal. But they're so busy . . . did they send for you? To help?"

"I—just came on my own," I said.

"Oh, gosh, what did you bring to eat?"

"Peanut butter and jelly."

"Sounds okay," Ellen said. She sank back against the pillow. I went over, got another pillow from the next bed, and placed it behind her so she could sit up. I handed her one of the sandwiches. She took a few bites.

"Anything to drink?" Ellen asked.

"I didn't bring anything," I said. "I can go back and get some juice. Or make tea, if I can figure out how to use the burners."

"Whatever," said Ellen, sinking down again. "I am thirsty. Very thirsty."

"Want water?" I asked.

"Tea would be better," she said faintly.

I made my way back to the lodge, to the kitchen, and after searching for several minutes I finally found a box of matches and a kettle and managed to boil water for tea. Finding tea bags was another major project. At last I discovered them in the pantry. By then the kettle was screaming from the stove, and I ran to stop it, to search out the mugs—the entire procedure must have taken me nearly half an hour. I felt exhausted, especially since the heat of midday was upon us.

Back in the cabin, Ellen was asleep. I sat down at the little wicker desk, where I had first seen Beatrice, the nurse, and I ate my peanut-butter-and-jelly sandwich, washing it down with tap water from a little paper cup.

At last Ellen awakened. She sat up again, and I gave her the tea. She made a face. "No sugar?"

I sighed. "I'll go get you some."

I ran back to the lodge for sugar, grumbling to myself. Back again, I gave Ellen the sugar and sat by her bed, watching her drink the tea, which by now had to be barely warm.

Thank God, Ellen didn't complain; I wouldn't have known how to contain myself. Nursing, I decided, is the pits. I didn't see how Ruth could stand it.

"Did you have chicken pox?" Ellen asked.

"Yes. I was about seven. It was awful. I itched all over and couldn't scratch."

"Did you have a high fever?"

"No."

"I did," Ellen said rather proudly. "My fever went up to a hundred and three. Any higher, and they would have had to take me to the hospital."

I wished they had, but I didn't say so. "How come you didn't go home?" I asked.

It was a mistake. A look flashed across Ellen's face, sardonic and bitter. "What home?"

"What do you mean? Everybody has a home."

"I live with my sister. She works. She's got three kids. It's a madhouse. They don't need a sick person to add to it."

The question burned in my mouth—what about your parents? It wasn't my business. If Ellen wanted me to know, she'd tell me. I burned with curiosity, but remembered my manners and kept silent.

It was difficult to look at Ellen's face and compare her now to the time I'd first seen her, looking absolutely gorgeous, all smiles and bouncy, leading the entire camp in song.

I went to the windows and pulled aside all the draperies. The room brightened immediately. I pushed open two of the windows. "You need fresh air," I said. "And I'll make your bed."

"I don't want to move."

"You can stay in it," I said. "Just turn on your side when I tell you."

While Ellen turned, I pulled taut first one side of the sheets, then the other. I pulled back the top sheet, shook it slightly to air, then did the same with the blankets, before smoothing them over Ellen again and tucking them lightly in.

Ellen sighed. "Where'd you learn to do that?"

"My sister's a nursing student. She showed me, she practiced on me in the bed. She also showed me how to give a bed bath."

"Oh, no, you don't!" Ellen exclaimed, drawing back.

"I'll go get a pan of water. You should at least wash your hands and face. I can wash your feet and your back. You'll feel a lot better."

"I'm not washing with that cold water," Ellen said. "Not on your life."

"I'll get warm water from the bathroom in there," I said, nodding toward the lavatory. "Unless you want to get up and go in there and wash."

"I'm too weak," Ellen said.

I gave her a quick glance. "All right," I said. "Bed bath, then."

I had never washed another person, except for the hands of the little children when I baby-sat. This was different. This was an intimacy, and a kind of giving I had not experienced before. Always, I was the recipient. When I was little, Mother or Lisa use to bathe me and shampoo my hair. Lisa still did my hair sometimes, for fun, washing and styling it, even cutting the ends and the bangs.

Ellen, her face puffed and red, with sores all over her legs and arms, was an unattractive patient. But as I washed her arms and her feet, then gently patted her dry, I discovered that she was suddenly important to me.

When she was settled again, Ellen smiled slightly. "I do feel better," she said. "Who took care of you when you had chicken pox?"

"My mother." I remembered, she had stayed home from work for three days nursing me, and she had slept beside my bed at night.

"My mom's dead," Ellen said. "Daddy, too. There was an accident on a train, and they were killed. I was eight. My big sister was eighteen, thank goodness, or I would have had to go to an orphanage. So my sister took care of me. She got me clothes and food, and she made me do my homework. But she never talked to me much, you know?"

I nodded. "I have an older sister like that. Ruth. She never played with me or laughed and fooled around, like my other sister does. Ruth's a nurse. She's hardly ever around. But she likes to take care of sick people. Maybe it's too hard for her to get close to us—I don't know why."

Ellen nodded. "Are you going to be a nurse?" she asked.

"Oh, no," I quickly said. "I'm going to be a vet. Or a teacher. Or a writer. I'm not good with sick people."

Ellen smiled again. "Take it from me," she said, "I've seen much worse. I think I'll get some sleep now."

I stayed with Ellen for a little while, rearranging the

magazines on the shelves and dusting with a cloth I found in the closet.

Then I took her teacup back to the kitchen, where Sal was standing before the stove, wearing a large white apron, stirring something in an enormous pot.

"Stew," she said as I entered. "For tonight. If you have a minute, you could peel some potatoes and carrots for me."

"Sure," I said. "Where's Mary?"

"Up at the cabin. She'd like you there by two, if you don't mind. She has to leave for town, and you could watch Alice for her. Okay?"

"Sure," I said again, though I felt weary and hot and wanted only to take a quick dip in the lake, and had hoped that afterward I could run down to the stable and see Molly and the other animals.

Instead, Sal rummaged through several bins and brought out twelve potatoes, as many carrots, and some beans. "Here, thanks a million, Annie. You can cut everything up and add it to the stew and let it all simmer. Gosh, we're sure lucky you arrived when you did!"

Glumly I nodded. "Glad to be of service," I said sarcastically.

Sal only smiled and said cheerily, "So long, then!"

Having finished the vegetables, I went to Alice and stayed with her all afternoon. We played countless games of fish. I read to her, took her to the bathroom, dabbed her blisters with calamine lotion. Still, she whined and complained and cried; "Oooo, it's so awful! I itch all over! I'm going to scratch, I don't *care*."

"Don't scratch, don't you dare," I'd said, glowering at

Alice. Then I tried to placate her. "If you don't scratch, I'll play another game of fish."

"I don't want to play fish. I hate fish."

"We'll play dolls. Does your mom have any scraps? We can make doll clothes."

I remembered all the times Lisa had placated me thus, when I was sick in bed, or when Mama and Papa were working late, and I was lonely and tired and unhappy. I remembered the treats she cooked for me. I felt as if I'd switched roles as I asked Alice, "How about some chocolate pudding. Do you like chocolate pudding?"

"Mmm!" Alice beamed. "I love chocolate pudding."

"Does your mom have any I can fix?"

"Sure! She never fixes it though, not for a long time. She's always too busy. She never makes me anything nice," said Alice, pouting.

I thought, How unfair little kids are. Mary's a wonderful mother. I said, "Well, you wait a few minutes, and I'll go fix it."

In the kitchen I found the ingredients and a pan and cooked the pudding. The smell of warm chocolate brought back pleasant memories—of Mama's special concoction, chocolate soup, which is our family favorite, especially with the tiny macaroons that Mama makes.

I made the pudding and poured it into four small bowls. At home, Lisa usually did the cooking; I licked the pot, then soaked it. Now I did it all, as well as scrubbing out the pot and putting it away. As I stood in Mary's kitchen, looking out to the pine trees, for the first time in my life it struck me that someday I would have a home of my own, a kitchen of my own, and quite probably a child. I'd cook for her. I'd play with her and take care of her when she was sick. And she'd love me, adore me, want to be with me all the time, and I would love her and kiss her and want her with me. . . .

Suddenly I shuddered.

Alice and I ate the pudding. Then I cleaned the bowls and made Alice's bed and played two more games of fish and a game of paper dolls.

When Mary came home she looked exhausted and pale. I must have looked tired, too, for she put her arm around my shoulder and said, "Sit down, Annie, let's have a glass of lemonade. You look all done in."

"I think I should call my parents," I said.

"Sounds like a good idea," Mary said.

"I should not have run away like that," I said.

"I know," Mary said. "What do you think you want to do about it?"

"I'll go home in the morning," I said. "The same way I came. Maybe Ed could drive me to the village to the bus."

"I'm sure he'll be glad to," said Mary with a smile.

14

New Beginnings

THE BUS FOR L.A. DIDN'T LEAVE UNTIL THE AFTERNOON. I had this morning at Quaker Pines, maybe my last morning ever. I awakened early, with a sense of foreboding. Ellen was still asleep in the last bed against the wall. In sleep, she looked very pale and childlike. Her face had a tight, pinched look that reminded me somehow of Nancy Rae.

Nancy Rae. Every time I thought of her, I felt queasy. My mother had a saying which now came back to me: The person you wronged will eventually forget it, but you never will. Somehow Nancy Rae was more vivid to me now than any of my other cabin mates, even Tally. Why? Because something in those cold gray eyes had chilled me. Hating herself and her life, Nancy Rae hated back. What she wanted was love. Now I knew it.

It was very early yet, barely dawn. But I pulled on my jeans, shirt, and jacket and hurried down to the stable. The smell of the hay, damp with early morning dew, is the sweetest scent I have ever known. The pine trees were hung with dew; blossoms on the wild vines looked ready to explode with color.

Molly stood out in the ring, along with John's favorite, the Appaloosa named Bridie. Molly turned her head inquisitively as I approached; I saw her nostrils flare. Then she nodded her magnificent head up and down. She knew me.

I went to her, put my arms around her sleek neck, and as I stood very close to her, feeling her muscular body and that great heat that horses emanate, I felt overcome with emotions, both happiness and sorrow. Sorrow for all the people who never knew a moment like this, for wickedness, my own included, and happiness for being in a world with mornings like this one.

Mama was right; I couldn't forget Nancy Rae. I'd never forget her, because I had wronged her. As I stroked Molly's noble head, I thought about animals and people, the differences. We can choose, I thought, and sometimes we choose wrong. My parents had committed a terrible wrong against Tally and me, but so had I done wrong to Nancy Rae. I could not make it up to Nancy Rae. She was out of my life forever. It was different with my parents. I could go back now and they would forgive me, because they loved me. That's how it is with families. We can love each other over and over again, forgive each other over and over again. And we must do this, even though it is hard.

For the rest of the morning I helped Mary look after Alice. I played the piano for her, and we sang and made some dresses for her doll.

When I went to see Ellen in the infirmary, she was sitting up in bed, reading one of my favorite books, *A Girl of the*

Limberlost. It was I who had left the book there when Mary lent it to me; it seemed like many months ago. I realized it was only six weeks.

"Hi, looks like you're feeling better," I said.

"I am. Thanks. You're a good nurse. Have you read this book?" Ellen asked.

"Yes. Lots of times."

"Poor Elnora, to be shunned by her own mother like that! She's so cruel."

"Read on," I said. "The mother had her own reasons."

"What reasons? How can she be so mean to her own daughter?"

"Well, she blames Elnora for the father's death—it's not logical, but that's how people are sometimes. They get hurt, and then they take it out on the wrong person, someone completely innocent, like Elnora."

Ellen nodded. "You read a lot, don't you?"

"Yes. I love to read."

"I guess that's what makes you so smart."

I felt a sudden jolt. "Me?" I laughed. Then I remembered what Mary had taught me. "Thank you," I said.

Saying farewell to Mary was hard. I made it brief. "I'm not sure whether I can come for the next session," I said. "I'll have to ask my folks."

Mary nodded. "I understand."

"Thank you for wanting me, Mary."

"It wasn't only me," she said. "We voted. The entire staff, including junior counselors. You won, hands down."

My eyes must have been shining, because Mary laughed and said, "Including John Wright. You're a good camper, Annie. And a good friend."

We smiled at each other, and I hopped into the truck and
Ed took off.

The way home on the bus seemed shorter than the way
out. I did not want to go home, but I knew it was right.
Whatever happened, I had to face it. I pondered the consequences. Probably no phone calls. No friends coming over.
Maybe I'd be forbidden to leave the house at all. Isolated
there, what would I do all day, especially after having
known freedom? I imagined various scenarios, Papa yelling,
Mama refusing to speak to me for days. I imagined accusations and arguments, tears and threats, an uneasy peace
at last, the house silent, but with those terrible echoes of
anger.

I longed for Lisa back in our room, for Ruth still at
home, though she didn't talk to me much and often seemed
preoccupied. I wanted the three of us to be the way we were
when I was little, all together, always entangled in some
happening or other, good or bad—at least we were together.
Now I missed that.

It suddenly struck me. I wasn't the only one.

I knew, as if I'd stood in their shoes, that my parents
missed it, too, missed it terribly. That was what the fighting
was about—time was pulling us apart in different directions.
And they had already lost too much.

I was tired and stiff by the time the bus pulled into the
station. I dragged out my duffel bag, and as I stood in the
bus waiting to move out, to my great surprise, I saw my
parents standing in the middle of the station, Mama holding
Papa's arm.

They looked so out of place that I almost gasped. From

that distance I saw them like strangers, looking bewildered, people suddenly abandoned in a strange land.

Papa was dressed in dark slacks and his usual dress shoes; Mother wore her blue-and-white-print dress and a dab of lipstick. I could see she had done her hair up in curlers.

Even from this distance Papa looked tired. There were pouches under his eyes, and his shoulders were stooped, perhaps from carrying bundles of coats on his back. Did he always look this way? In my mind I conjured him up as I desired him to be, energetic and robust, athletic, full of fun and wit—yes, he was witty and often energetic, but he was also frail and his hair, at the sides, was gray.

I came down the ramp. Mother saw me. Her face broke into a smile so warm, so joyous, that I ran to her, flung my arms around her; and as we embraced, Papa kept saying, "Now, now, now, stop crying, for heaven's sake. Now, now, come to the car."

They spoke to me in German. How was the bus ride? Did I eat along the way? Where was my suitcase? The language fell on my ears like swift blows. People stared. I felt self-conscious.

The woman who had sold me my ticket was there behind the counter. This time her nose was not in a book. She looked up, caught my eye, and gave me a wink. I smiled back. She seemed to know everything; somehow, her wink implied that what I was going through was all pretty normal.

We drove home without saying much; we looked at streets and houses and Mama pointed out things like stores and dogs and children, as if she were a tour guide. I knew she, too, dreaded a confrontation.

Home, Papa told me, "Come into the kitchen. We will eat something."

Mother made tea, and she cut a fresh pound cake into thick slices and brought it to the table.

I went to bring plates and forks and milk. It felt odd to be here in our own kitchen; it was tiny by comparison to the camp kitchen, and I was moving too fast for this space, as if I had outgrown it.

Papa came in from washing his hands and sat down on the built-in bench. He sipped his tea, broke off some cake, and began to nibble.

"Take a whole piece on your plate, Arthur," Mama chided. "You always eat a whole piece or two—why do you pick at it? *Put it on your plate*."

With a submissive nod, Papa took the piece of cake onto his plate. He picked up his fork, speared a small bite. "Your mother," he said, his eyes twinkling, "is a real lady. Makes us watch our manners. I'm afraid," he said, "sometimes I am a"—he squinted, seeking the right word—"a roughneck."

I stared at him, not knowing what to say. Never in my life had I heard my father even hint at an apology. I held my breath.

"So," he said, spearing another bite of cake. "At this camp, you are taking care of horses?"

"Yes, Papa."

"This woman, this Mary, your mother talked to her. Your mother says she sounds like a good person."

"She's a wonderful person, Papa."

"So, this wonderful person, Mary, says you should come back and help out there, with the little children. You like helping with the little children?"

"Oh, yes, Papa."

Mother came to the table. She sipped her tea. Her eyes

looked red rimmed. She was watching me and Papa, her eyes darting back and forth between us. I did not actually see this, for I, too, kept my gaze upon my father, but I knew.

"Just like your mama," he said. "She also likes to take care of little children. Horses, I don't know. Have you ever sat on a horse, Margo?"

"Once," said my mother. She pursed her lips, smiled in spite of herself. "It was the same year I met you. We went out to the country, my brother and his wife and I."

Her brother, my uncle Harry, I had never known, but I had heard him talked about. We had left them all behind in Germany.

"So, maybe you will try it again," said Papa.

"Go on," Mama scoffed, shaking her head, laughing. "Me on a horse?"

Papa lit a cigarette. Smoke floated above the three of us, like a mist. "This woman, Mary, said we can bring you. Next Sunday, the camp starts again. She said we could drive up there and see everything. It would make your mother feel better," he said, half glancing at me, "to see those people you are with. I know your mother. She worries."

I could not speak for the ache in my chest and throat.

He continued, as if somebody had argued. "So, if your mother doesn't need you home, what do I care? Next time you want something, you ask me. Are you afraid to ask your father?"

"I—no, Papa." But that wasn't true, either. Sometimes, I thought, a little lie hurts less than the truth.

Now I exclaimed, while new possibilities whirled in my mind, "You would really drive me to camp? You would come to see it, really? I could show you the cabins, the horses, the meadow, the lake. Could you really? How do you know how to get there? It's far, up the mountain, it's pretty hot. . . ."

"Listen," said Papa sternly, "I am not such a greenhorn that I cannot go in the car to the mountains. I have traveled all over the world!"

In that very moment, while joy began to flood through me, the telephone rang. It was Lisa.

"Are you going back?" she asked.

"Yes," I said.

"Are they taking you in the car?"

"Yes. Sunday."

"Well, glory be," said Lisa. "I'm glad. Maybe I can come, too. Will your friend, that girl from Florida, be there?"

I giggled. "Tallahassee. She's not *from* Florida. That's just her name. And no, she won't. I'm the only returning camper. But you'll meet Mary and Ellen and John and you'll see . . . oh, Lisa, I can't wait to show you everything."

From where I stood I could see into the kitchen. I saw Papa reach for Mama's hand across the table. It was a tender touch. To me, it meant a new beginning.

15

Epilogue

THEY ALL CAME IN THE CAR TO TAKE ME TO QUAKER PINES, even Ruth, and I remember the drive up into the mountains, for the first time sharing with my family the world of nature that I loved.

The deep green pine trees, the high, sheer peaks, and the running streams at the roadside, all seemed alive, seemed to hum to us with their own voices, so that when Papa turned on the radio, it was with a double sense of shock that we heard the words that in themselves seemed to explode upon us.

"The United States has dropped an atomic bomb on the Japanese town of Hiroshima. The blast of that single bomb was greater than any force ever before generated on this planet. The city of Hiroshima is destroyed. From the intense heat of the bomb, everything in a radius of four miles is totally vaporized. Early reports show over sixty thousand people dead and missing. . . ."

We heard other phrases, new words: "The dawn of the

nuclear age . . . the power of a thousand suns . . . harnessing the power of the universe . . . for total destruction . . . or for peace.''

We heard, but it was impossible to fathom it. I kept thinking about that word, *vaporized*. Weeks and months later, when the pictures came out in the newspapers, we saw and we trembled at the force that had turned steel girders into twisted sticks and had pulverized cars, buildings, and people alike. Later, too, we saw the mutilated bodies, the scarred faces, and in school we talked about possible beneficent uses for this awesome new power.

That day, however, as we drove higher into the mountains, we said very little. "Terrible," said my mother. "Terrible."

"Finally over," said Papa. "This war."

"You can imagine how many wounded!" cried Ruth. "And dead."

"If it ends the war," Mother said, "many lives will be saved on both sides."

I only sighed, thinking of Setsu, my friend, wondering how she and her parents might feel at this moment. They had family in Japan. I had never heard of a city called Hiroshima. A few days later we heard the name of another place where a second atomic bomb was dropped. Nagasaki. Both became etched in our minds forever.

"Well, we can't let it spoil everything," said Lisa. "I am sorry for those people, of course. But, well, they started the war. Remember, Pearl Harbor."

"If you had ever seen someone with burns," Ruth began heatedly, but Papa interrupted. "That's enough!"

Papa switched off the radio and lit a cigarette. He opened

the window. The breeze wafted in, bringing us the scent of the living forest. By and by we settled down, and I looked for birds and squirrels and green seedlings growing beside their parent trees.

At last we arrived, eager to be out and stretching. Lisa wore slacks, I wore my jeans, naturally. But Ruth had insisted on wearing high heels and a cream-colored linen dress. As she picked her way along the paths, Richard came by in his Jeep. Later he would tell us how he fell in love instantly; how he knew at that very moment that he wanted to marry her.

For Ruth, it took just a little longer.

Lisa finally did marry Nate. She got the house she wanted, and the babies; she never seemed to miss her dancing. She never regretted her choice.

I didn't see Tally again, though I thought of her often. Neither she nor Herbie came back to camp. Maybe they moved away. I often wonder what happens to the people we meet along the way, wishing we could remain friends forever.

My crush on John Wright did change to friendship. We were counselors together at Quaker Pines for several more years.

I remember knowing, by the end of that summer, some of the things I would do with the rest of my life—like teaching children and tending animals and writing stories. Like celebrating freedom, as we all did when at last, one August day, the war ended.

Richard had been listening to his radio nonstop for the past twenty-four hours, when suddenly he burst out of his cabin, ran to the lodge, and pulled the bell rope.

On and on the bell pealed, reaching campers everywhere, drawing them from the lake, the stable, the playing fields. I was in the crafts hut with the group of eight-year-olds. Mary had assigned me to help Ellen with them, and I slept in their cabin, too.

"Something's up," I told them. "Come on! Quick."

With little girls hanging on to my hands and arms, I rushed to the flagpole, where everyone assembled. In the center stood Richard, hoisting the flag, while John stood at attention. Beside him was Mary, with Alice, Sal, and Douglas. Douglas's hand was lifted in a salute.

Then Douglas spoke. "The war is over. We have a victory. The Japanese have surrendered. Thank God, the war is over."

With a beaming, broad smile, Ellen came forward. She held out her arms and announced the song: "God Bless America."

I gathered my little campers close around me. We all linked arms and made a large circle, swaying as we sang:

"God bless America
land that I love. . . ."

Then we sang my favorite: "One World."

And as I looked about at the faces of the campers and staff, many like me from distant lands, now standing together, it seemed definitely possible, a promise for the future.